# SOLDIER

## SECRET MISSION: GUAM

# DOGS

# READ ALL THE

# SOLDIER DOGS

## BOOKS!

# SOLDIER

## SECRET MISSION: GUAM

# DOGS

MARCUS SUTTER

ILLUSTRATIONS BY ANDIE TONG

**HARPER** FESTIVAL

*An Imprint of HarperCollinsPublishers*

*For the people of Guam and the Dobermans of World War II*

HarperFestival is an imprint of HarperCollins Publishers.

Soldier Dogs #3: Secret Mission: Guam
Copyright © 2019 by HarperCollins Publishers
Flag artwork on page iii, used under license from Shutterstock.com
Photos on pages 182 and 183, used under license from Shutterstock.com
Insert map artwork, used under license from Shutterstock.com
All rights reserved. Printed in the United States of America.

Library of Congress Control Number: 2018964881
ISBN 978-0-06-284407-1
Typography by Marisa Rother
19 20 21 22 23   PC/LSCH   10 9 8 7 6 5 4 3 2 1
❖
First Edition

# PROLOGUE

Enemy soldiers ran toward the field hospital. Bullets whined past the hiding spot where Stryker the war dog was crouching.

A mortar shell exploded nearby, digging chunks out of the earth. Stryker nudged the boy deeper into the hiding spot as dirt pelted his furry coat.

Stryker felt the urge to fight in his chest. He wanted to growl, but he'd been trained to stay quiet. His hackles raised as the enemy soldiers raced closer to him and the boy—and to the hospital behind them—but he didn't move.

He stayed with the boy called Bo.

Bo *hadn't* been trained. He didn't know about enemies or sneak attacks. The boy wasn't armed with a weapon—or even with teeth and claws. That's why Stryker needed to keep close.

Stryker felt his muscles tense. He'd wait here, hidden behind the fallen tree, until the enemy came near enough. Then he'd leap at them and show them what a war dog could do.

He felt Bo trembling beside him. That was okay. Humans got scared. Even marines got scared. Fear made humans' hearts beat faster and their eyes widen. It made their senses sharp and alert—almost as sharp and alert as a Doberman's.

Stryker was afraid that Bo would stand and fight despite his fear. He needed the boy to run. That was the only way he'd survive. The moment Stryker threw himself at the enemy, the boy needed to *flee*.

He needed to live.

Stryker nudged Bo's arm, telling him to get

ready to move. Bo could scramble through the hospital behind them, past the sickbeds and the bandaged patients—if he left now.

"Don't worry, boy," Bo whispered. "I'm right here."

Stryker nudged him again. He didn't know what those words meant, but he knew the boy wasn't getting ready to run.

"I-I'll take care of you," Bo said in a shaky voice.

Gunfire ripped into the other side of the tree, shredding the wood into splinters. Bo ducked his head, his black hair short and silky.

Pain stung Stryker's muzzle. He narrowed his eyes and gathered his rear legs to leap, tracking the enemy's position with his pointy ears. Rifles cracked and big navy guns boomed from the US ships offshore.

Stryker heard a scuffle and gasp of hand-to-hand fighting. He smelled bitter smoke and sweet gasoline.

The enemy was ten strides away before Stryker let himself make a sound. He snarled at the boy, telling him to run!

Bo grabbed a branch from the ground. "W-we almost made it," he said. "We almost made it."

Stryker growled. *Get moving!*

"You and me," Bo said, tears in his eyes. "Together till the end."

# CHAPTER 1

TWO DAYS EARLIER

**B**o hacked through the jungle undergrowth. His machete blade sliced through stalks and stems and vines.

Then it stuck in a thick branch.

Bo grunted in frustration. Sweat stung his eyes in the damp heat, and hunger flared in his empty stomach. Bugs buzzed his ears, but he was too tired to brush them away.

A beefy soldier barked at him in Japanese and a jolt of fear gave Bo strength. He jerked the machete free from the branch. His arms trembled, but he raised the blade again.

Up.

Down.

Up.

Down.

The rich scent of jungle vegetation surrounded Bo as the *crash* and *boom* of fighting rolled toward him from the western side of the island.

The American navy had started attacking more than two weeks earlier. Bo had heard thousands of shells exploding onto Guam every day, as the Americans fought to kick out the Japanese army that had taken over the island.

At first the huge ships and the buzzing airplanes slammed the Japanese positions for fifteen or twenty minutes every hour, softening them up before the invasion. Now the bombing never seemed to stop. Which meant the invasion was happening very soon—if it hadn't already started.

The Japanese forces were scared. Bo could tell. For the past week or so, soldiers had forced every male Chamorro between the ages of twelve and sixty to work for them. The Chamorros lived in labor camps; they dug trenches and cleared jungle

paths to prepare for the fight against the Americans. Anyone who disobeyed was tortured or punished with death.

Bo was a Chamorro—a native of the Mariana Islands—and he'd turned twelve the previous month. Lucky him.

His uncles and father had been sent to the west somewhere, closer to the action. His mother and older sister had been brought to a labor camp on the eastern side of the island, to provide food and material for the Imperial Japanese military. Bo wasn't exactly alone—he knew some men from his village—but being separated from his family scared him even more than the sound of bombs.

The big Japanese soldier lurking behind him didn't help. He was the one they called "Two Ears." Bo didn't understand the nickname, but for some reason it frightened him.

So he hacked through the jungle, ignoring the pain and the fear. His heart pounded. Sweat covered his skin as the sun lowered through the jungle canopy.

Two Ears walked away from him—but he kept returning, like a schoolyard bully.

Every time he returned, Bo's skin crawled. When he couldn't stand it any longer, he turned toward the soldier—and smiled. Trying to seem friendly and unthreatening.

"What are you smiling at?" Two Ears bellowed.

"N-nothing!" Bo said.

Two Ears stepped closer, grabbing Bo's shirt in his fist.

Bo saw the sharp angle of his cheekbones, the scars that ran along both ears. He raised his hands in surrender. "I'm sorry, please!"

# CHAPTER 2

**W**ith the breeze ruffling his fur, Stryker loped along beside Boomer, another war dog. Spent bullets littered the beach at the base of the thick jungle. The two Dobermans darted past fallen coconut trees, avoiding the craters left behind by bombs. They had a mission to complete.

Behind them, the ocean was packed with American warships. A few piles of metal lay in the shallow water, and Stryker could tell that Boomer didn't like the scent of them.

The twisted lumps of metal were the remains of the car-boats that had carried marines onto the island. When the marines first landed, the Japanese had been waiting for them. They'd blown up many of the marines' car-boats.

Now that the marines had taken over this stretch of beach, things weren't so bad. But Boomer had lost some of his humans on the first day of fighting. He'd come through without injuries, but he still whimpered in his sleep and moved his paws, trying to outrun the enemy shells.

When that happened, Stryker licked Boomer's ears to calm him. It was the least he could do for a fellow warrior.

The enemy soldiers had been pushed back from the beach. They'd retreated past the hills into the jungle. Every inch of distance had cost the marines blood and tears. And the daily battles never let up.

Stryker picked up the pace when he caught a whiff of his pack of marines. That's where he was headed. He led Boomer past the demolished beach, toward the battlefront in the jungle. They were on a mission.

In the distance, gunfire sounded along with the faraway *whoosh* of a flamethrower. Boomer must've sensed they were safe, because he shot ahead, his stubby tail wagging in a dare.

Boomer wanted to race, did he?

Stryker and Boomer zigzagged toward the jungle. They'd been trained to run like that, so the enemy sharpshooters couldn't shoot them.

Stryker knew that he'd never beat Boomer in a fight . . . but Boomer would never beat *him* in a race. And sure enough, Stryker soon overtook the bigger dog. It was all about speed, not power!

Stryker barked in triumph as they split up. He veered to the left while Boomer raced to the right.

Stryker was heading deeper into the jungle to bring his person, Dawson, a response to a message. Boomer was delivering ammunition to *his* person, Ramirez, in a different part of the jungle. They were both running closer to the battlefront.

Stryker sniffed the air as he zigzagged into the jungle path. Finding Dawson's scent was easy for a Doberman. Even back when he'd been a house dog, Stryker could've tracked a mouse through a herd of horses.

He didn't hesitate—even when a shell exploded behind him. He kept running until he found Dawson and the other marines sheltering behind a thick stand of trees.

"Good dog," Dawson told him, giving Stryker's head a quick scratch before removing the message from his collar pouch.

Stryker leaned against Dawson's leg. *Good human.*

When Dawson read the message, his shoulders stiffened and his jaw clenched. Apparently Stryker had raced through enemy fire to bring his marines bad news. Either that, or a dangerous mission.

# CHAPTER 3

**B**o froze. His throat was dry, and his heart was pounding.

Two Ears shook him and laughed, enjoying his fear.

Bo wanted to run away. To scream or curse or fight. But he just stood there shaking, his shirt crumpled in the Japanese soldier's fist. He'd seen what happened to brave resisters. He'd seen what happened to anyone the Japanese even suspected of opposing them.

So he didn't move, too afraid to do anything except pray.

After a few seconds, Two Ears shoved Bo aside and snarled at him to get in line with the others.

Usually after a day's work, the soldiers would order the Chamorro men and boys to return to their camp, where Bo would hug his knees and try not to cry. But things were different today. Today, the soldiers made them march through the jungle for no reason.

Which made Bo even more afraid. Everyone knew that if the Japanese took you into the jungle, you might never come back out.

"Keep moving!" one said in Japanese, gesturing roughly.

"He wants us to keep going," Bo translated.

Most of the other Chamorros didn't speak much Japanese. Bo knew a little. After the Japanese Imperial Army invaded Guam a few years earlier, they'd made every child on the island take classes with Japanese teachers. The teachers had made the kids learn the language, along with patriotic songs. And they'd made them praise the Japanese emperor every single day.

But Bo was Chamorro. Guam had become a US territory a long time ago: back in 1898, after the Spanish-American War. Bo had grown up reading American books and listening to American music, but even so, Bo was Chamorro through and through.

Then on December 10, 1941, just three days after Japan attacked Pearl Harbor, Japanese troops landed on Guam. They'd imprisoned the US Marines stationed there and ordered two Chamorro men to lower the American flag and raise the Japanese one.

The men refused.

So the Japanese executed them. And they made sure no Chamorro would forget it.

Bo hadn't forgotten. He'd *never* forget that.

"Get moving!" the Japanese soldier snapped. "You're not heading back to base tonight!"

"We're not going back tonight," Bo explained to the others.

"Where are we going?" a guy named Luis asked him. He was a broad-shouldered eighteen-year-old with a sweet face.

"I don't know," Bo said. The truth was, he was

afraid to ask. If you asked the soldiers anything they didn't like, they would beat you—or worse.

The Japanese soldiers shouted commands and threats, forcing the Chamorros farther into the jungle along a narrow dirt path.

After ten minutes, Luis quietly asked a soldier where they were going.

The soldier slapped Luis's face hard enough to make his mouth bleed.

Then Two Ears pointed his rifle at Luis. His finger shifted to the trigger, and Bo's heart stopped. He wanted to do something, he wanted to *say* something. He wanted to be brave and unafraid, but the Japanese killed anyone who was brave.

Two Ears's finger tightened on the trigger.

His knuckles whitened.

He was about to fire!

# CHAPTER 4

Stryker listened for the enemy while his person, Dawson, read the message. "We need to take the next hill, through the trees. They say the Japanese already abandoned their position."

A scruffy-cheeked marine peered into the distance. "I guess we'll see if they're right."

"C'mere, boy." Dawson clipped the leash to Stryker's collar. That meant it was time to patrol.

Stryker led his pack forward. He padded through the jungle, sniffing for land mines and listening for any motion or danger. The nine humans formed a ragged line behind him.

Then a small, crater-scarred field opened between him and the jungle hill where Dawson was heading. Open spaces were dangerous. There was no cover except for a half-fallen wooden fence.

Stryker continued forward, every sense alert.

The pack followed. Not exactly scared, but . . . tense.

Stryker heard a man in the trees at the far end of the clearing. Two men. Maybe more, hidden in the branches.

Stryker alerted silently, pointing his snout and pricking his ears. *Danger! A threat to the pack! Enemy soldiers!*

Dawson knew exactly what he meant and gestured crisply. The other marines threw themselves sideways, taking cover behind the fence.

At the same moment, the enemy soldiers fired!

Bullets ripped through the air. An enemy soldier shouted, and Stryker scrambled to safety behind the fence.

Dawson pulled him close and pressed his forehead to Stryker's. "You keep saving our lives."

Stryker licked his chin.

"Except now we're pinned down," the scruffy-cheeked marine said.

"We can crawl along the fence into the jungle," said the marine who led the pack. "Take them from the flank."

"That won't work. They'll know we're on the move."

Dawson looked toward the enemy hidden in the trees. "Not if some of us stay here and make noise."

"Too obvious. You think they won't know *why* some of us are here flapping our lips?"

"Who said anything about lips?" Dawson asked, and gave Stryker a silent hand command.

Stryker barked.

"Oh!" the marine said. "You'll stay here with the dog?"

Stryker barked again and then growled, but Dawson kept gesturing, which meant he wanted something else. Stryker whimpered and yelped. Yeah, that's what Dawson wanted! Whimpers and yelps.

"They'll think they hit him," Dawson said. "And I'll give 'em something to shoot at."

"Good plan," the leader said. "Stay here. Keep your head down and your mouth open."

The other marines started belly-crawling along the fence, their scraping and jangling muffled by the battle sounds.

"What'm I supposed to say?" Dawson asked Stryker, giving him another hand signal. "Well, here we are on Guam. It's a long way from Minnesota. I guess being a marine's not so different from being a fireman, though."

Stryker yowled a little.

"Putting out fires all across the world." Dawson glanced at Stryker. "You remind me of my German shepherd a little. That's why they put us together. I trained Chief, so they picked me for a dog handler."

Stryker yelped sharply.

"What, you want me to stick to the point?"

Stryker yelped again.

"Fine. Guam. Uh, it's a tiny island in the Pacific." Dawson poked his rifle barrel over the

top of the fence—and enemy bullets chunked into the wood on the other side. "Never thought you'd end up here, did you?"

Stryker whined.

"Me either." Dawson crawled a little farther and raised his rifle again. He was making it look like the whole pack was still here, not just two of them. "But Guam is important. For two reasons."

Stryker gave two yelps, keeping one ear cocked in case the enemy came closer.

"That's right. Two." Dawson fired a wild shot toward the jungle. "One is that Guam is a little over sixteen hundred miles from Japan. This is just a little island, but it's a big deal. Once we get an air base here, we can bring the war to the Japanese home islands."

At Dawson's hand gesture, Stryker whined.

"And the second reason is, when the Japanese invaded Guam, they took over a marine barracks on the island." A hard note entered Dawson's voice. "Now we're taking it back."

Stryker barked.

"Though first we—" A barrage of enemy gunfire interrupted him.

Bullets slammed into the other side of the fence.

*Crack! Crack!* The worn wood shuddered and split.

With a dull *snap*, a fence board broke. There was nothing between Dawson and the enemy bullets.

# CHAPTER 5

**B**o watched in horror as Two Ears spun his rifle and slugged Luis in the face with the butt. "No questions!" he barked.

Luis stumbled a few steps, blood dripping from his mouth. Nobody else asked where they were going.

The Chamorro men and boys just walked along, hunched and afraid, until the dirt path joined with a wider road. That's when Bo heard the murmur of voices. Hundreds of voices. More Chamorros, packing the road. Men and women, young and old.

They looked dusty and tired, wearing tattered clothes. And they were being forced to keep marching by more Japanese soldiers.

With his heart in his throat, Bo joined the crowd stumbling along the road. He looked for his family—his parents or sister or even just his cousins—but he didn't see any familiar faces.

The group was heading southward. Most of them were walking—or limping—but some rode in carts pulled by carabao or water buffalo. Nobody knew where they were going except the Japanese soldiers riding in a military car called a Yonki.

Then Bo spotted his mother.

She was standing with her back turned, huddled close to a bunch of other Chamorros. Warmth spread in his chest as he ran to her.

"Mom!" he said, grabbing her arm. "Mom!"

But when the woman turned, she wasn't Bo's mother. She didn't even look that much like her. Tears sprang to Bo's eyes. He wanted to give up, right there. He wanted to fall to the ground and never take another step.

"I'm sorry." The woman pressed a small hard papaya into Bo's hand. "Here. Your mom would

want you to have this."

A Yonki horn blared, and a Japanese soldier yelled, "Keep moving! No talking!"

The crowd scattered—it was rare that an Imperial Japanese soldier only gave a warning. Bo lost sight of the woman in the chaos but almost bumped into Luis.

"Are you okay?" Bo asked.

"Just banged up," Luis said, his voice slurred from his bloody lip. "Did they say where they're leading us?"

"Not that I heard."

"Stick close to them and see if you can overhear anything."

Bo didn't want to get too close to the Japanese soldiers. He wanted to be brave like Luis, though, so he said, "Okay."

As he inched closer, he could hear them talking, but he couldn't make out most of the words. His Japanese was just schoolroom stuff.

The Chamorros marched for hours, until the sun set through the trees. The old and the weak struggled, but they were too afraid of getting beaten to fall behind.

Bo saw a girl about his age, carrying a baby on her hip and holding a toddler's hand. She looked exhausted, with her hair plastered to her sweaty cheeks. Still, she tried to smile every time she looked down at the toddler.

By that time, Bo's feet were aching and his stomach throbbed with hunger. He felt like he was about to collapse, and he wasn't even holding a baby! He didn't know how the girl was still standing.

He staggered forward until he caught up with her. "Do you want me to look after one of the little ones?"

She eyed him warily. She didn't answer for five or six steps. The baby's head bobbed against her chest. "No. Thank you."

The toddler tugged her arm. "I'm hungry."

"I know, *neni*," the girl said.

Bo didn't say anything for a minute. Then he gave the girl the papaya he'd tucked into his shirt. "Here, for your brother."

"My sister," the girl said. "Thanks."

Bo nodded.

"I'm Teresita," the girl said.

"Ramón," he told her. "I'm from outside Agat. Everyone calls me Bo."

She told him where she was from, a little village that he'd barely heard of. She said that she'd been in the fields the previous day when the Japanese rounded up everyone in her village and started them marching.

"I lost my parents," she told him.

Bo didn't know if she meant that they'd died, and he was afraid to ask. Maybe she just couldn't find them.

After a few feet, the toddler took Bo's hand. Bo squeezed back. He was still hungry and afraid, but at least he wasn't alone.

# CHAPTER 6

Another fence board snapped in half!

Stryker leaped at Dawson. He knocked his human away from the bullets, putting himself in the line of fire.

The rounds tracked closer. One smashed into a broken board two strides from Stryker. Three more dug holes in the ground right in front of his paws and—

The enemy fire stopped at the blast of grenades on the other side of the field. The rest of the marine pack had reached the Japanese!

"Stupid dog," Dawson said, pulling Stryker to safety. "Don't *do* that."

Stryker wagged, enjoying the praise—then listened carefully. It sounded like his pack had won the fight.

By the time he and Dawson joined the other marines, the enemy soldiers were all gone.

"If they'd caught us in the open," the deep-voiced marine said, "it would've been curtains."

The scruffy-cheeked marine slapped the leader on the back. "You still think the mutt's a waste of rations?"

"He can eat my dinner any day," the leader said. "Good boy, Stryker. Good boy!"

Stryker ignored him. He had work to do. At Dawson's command, he scouted deeper into the jungle. Ears pricked and nostrils flaring, he prowled toward the top of the hill Dawson and the rest of the pack needed to claim.

The jungle muffled the sound of battle. A warm breeze brought a scent that reminded Stryker of fresh-cut grass, of a lawnmower growling in front of a tidy house, of wrestling in the yard with his boy. Stryker remembered his first home, the family that raised him as a puppy before he'd joined the military.

But he wasn't a puppy anymore. He tilted his head toward a faint scent coming from a tangled thicket. It smelled like the traces that remained after the enemy left—except why was it coming from a thicket?

"What's wrong?" the scruffy-cheeked marine whispered to Dawson.

"I don't know. He usually sits for a land mine and points for enemy soldiers."

"Send him in."

"He's not trained to flush out the enemy."

"Saving our butts is his job," the pack leader said.

Dawson took a breath. "Yeah."

Stryker didn't understand the words, but he guessed Dawson was trying to protect him. Which was silly. In a fight, you don't protect your strongest pack member.

You use him.

And that's what Dawson did. He gestured, telling Stryker to enter the thicket.

Stryker didn't hesitate—even when pointy

leaves and sharp twigs snagged his coat and scratched his nose. He crouched low and pushed forward, toward the scent.

After a minute, he found a sheet of paper caught on a thorny bush that smelled like the enemy. Stryker didn't know exactly what Dawson wanted, so he decided to fetch. He grabbed the paper in his mouth and crawled back to his pack.

"It's a map!" Dawson said.

"Looks recent," the pack leader said. "Too bad I don't read Japanese."

"You barely read *English*," the scruffy-cheeked marine said.

When the men laughed, Stryker heard their relief. They had taken the hill without losing anyone—*yet*.

# CHAPTER 7

**B**o stumbled along the road with Teresita. His arms ached from holding the sleeping toddler to his shoulder. His eyes felt gritty from exhaustion.

Still, he kept walking until a bright light washed across him from up ahead.

Headlights.

Japanese soldiers shouted, and a jolt of fear roused Bo from his daze. "What's happening?" he asked.

"They say we're here," Teresita said.

"Where?"

"Just . . . here."

As Bo passed the line of Yonkis, he heard the murmur of voices. When his eyes adjusted to the moonlit jungle, he couldn't believe the sight in front of him.

Thousands of Chamorros packed the area. They'd been forced to gather in this jungle valley, and some of them looked like they'd been there for days, or even weeks.

Families huddled miserably together. Some slept beneath carts or in makeshift tents made from tangantangan branches and coconut leaves.

The whole place was teeming with people. It reminded Bo of the ants he'd find beneath a damp log. And around them all, Japanese soldiers patrolled, keeping everyone in place.

Bo felt suddenly sick. "Why? Why take us all here?"

"You saw the American planes last month," a voice said behind him.

Bo spun. "Luis!"

"And you heard the American navy pounding the Japanese defenses," Luis continued. "The

Japanese are rounding us up because they're afraid we'll rise up and join the Americans."

"They're right to be afraid," Teresita said.

Bo didn't want to say that *he* was afraid, too. Instead, he sat with the kids while Teresita and Luis stripped leaves from a tree. He helped them make a small, unsteady lean-to, then they all crowded inside. At least they were out of the drizzle.

"I'm hungry," the little one said. "And the baby needs a banana."

"We all need bananas," Teresita said, taking the sleeping infant from Bo.

When the rain slacked, Bo heard voices all around the lean-to speaking in Chamorro. The sound soothed him—until two rifle shots echoed across the encampment.

A terrified silence fell.

Even the wind seemed to hold its breath, waiting for more shots.

Bo felt his empty stomach clench . . . but nothing happened.

Eventually, Luis crawled outside to gather more leaves for their shelter. The baby woke and

cried from hunger. Teresita rocked her while she told the toddler a story.

Bo went to look for his family. He liked Teresita and Luis, but he *needed* his mom and dad—or even just his sister.

He wandered through the camp, amazed by the size of the crowd—young and old, weak and strong, sick and healthy. All without food, without shelter, surrounded by armed guards in the jungle.

He didn't find his parents.

He saw two of his sister's friends, though. His sister was shy, but her friends were loud and bold. Except now they were shaking and crying. That scared Bo so much that he scurried away without speaking to them.

Bo searched for his family for an hour before he gave up.

Sniffling a little, he retraced his steps through the dark camp to the lean-to with Luis and Teresita. They made room for him and didn't ask if he'd found his parents. They already knew the answer.

# CHAPTER 8

After the pack finished securing the hilltop, Dawson and Stryker backtracked to their base with the map they'd found. They carefully made their way down the hill and across the jungle to the beach again with Stryker in the lead.

"You're some dog," Dawson said. "Hunting down enemy documents."

Stryker twitched one ear, recognizing the tone as warm but not urgent.

"Unless it's actually a shopping list."

Stryker glanced at Dawson. Humans did so

much pointless yapping!

"Or a takeout menu," Dawson continued, scratching Stryker's head.

Stryker licked Dawson's wrist, and he smelled everywhere Dawson had been since waking up that morning.

"Those D-rations aren't quite cutting it," Dawson said.

Stryker led his yapping person along a track that stank of gasoline and tanks. In a few minutes they had reached the bustling base where marines shouted and jogged, slept and ate.

Dawson left Stryker in a stuffy tent with Boomer and Ramirez and went to report about the map.

Stryker gave the air a quick sniff. Ramirez smelled of stale sweat and singed hair. Lying beside him, Boomer smelled satisfied. He gave his stumpy tail a few smug wags when Stryker approached. He must've delivered the message and kept his people safe.

Stryker plopped down beside Boomer and panted loudly, letting his tongue loll out of his mouth. *He'd* spotted an ambush, fetched a map, and kept his people safe.

Boomer rolled onto his side and pressed a paw against Stryker's leg.

Stryker nudged Boomer and gave him a friendly nuzzle hello. Even in the sweat-and-mud-scented tent, Boomer's scent changed to one of warm friendship and unquestioned trust.

Stryker knew that his own scent carried the same message, and when Ramirez offered food, he and Boomer ate together, shoulder to shoulder.

When Dawson returned from delivering the map, he checked Stryker's paws for cuts or scratches, then ran his hands over Stryker's coat. Dawson's tongue was so stubby that he needed to use his fingers to groom his packmates.

Silly human.

Finally, Dawson crawled into his fabric den to sleep while Stryker lay outside, his muzzle on his forepaw, alert for any danger.

The stink of gunpowder in the air didn't alarm him. The shells exploding in the south and the machine gun firing on the other side of the ridge didn't bother him either.

They were dangers, but not immediate ones.

His people were safe behind him in case the enemy mounted a surprise attack.

They knew he'd hear anything long before they would. He'd *smell* the enemy before the humans even heard them. Then he'd warn them.

His people slept easy, knowing Stryker was on the job.

Star shells burst overhead, turning the dark night to daylight. Stryker kept his gaze down. He didn't need light. He dozed, though he knew he'd wake at the sound of danger, even one too soft for humans to hear.

And sure enough, a few hours before dawn, Stryker heard the jingle of gear—weapons and a canteen. Footsteps ran closer, quick and intent.

Then a stranger burst into sight—heading straight for Dawson's tent.

# CHAPTER 9

Unfamiliar faces loomed around Bo in the pre-dawn gloom of the encampment. A cold mist drifted between the leafless coconut trees and the ramshackle lean-tos. The gurgle of the river sounded like sobbing.

Bo rubbed his neck as he passed an exhausted-looking father rocking a child in his arms. Just past him, two women crouched around the embers of a forbidden fire, trying to cook something. They glanced at Bo nervously; there wasn't enough food for their own family, and they were afraid he'd ask them to share.

He didn't.

He stumbled past, yawning. He'd woken a few minutes earlier, damp and tired and achy. Then he'd disentangled himself from Teresita's sister and headed outside. He needed to pee.

He crossed the camp, stunned by the sheer number of people the Japanese had crammed into the river valley. There were thousands of them, without food, without shelter, surrounded by armed guards.

Bo slipped between lean-tos and carts, creeping around the slumped forms sleeping in the open. Snores and weeping rose around him.

At the edge of the camp, he spotted two sentries leaning against a tree. Just standing there, watching the Chamorros. Making sure that nobody tried to escape the camp. Even though they weren't doing anything, Bo scurried onward until they couldn't see him.

There were more sentries in the jungle, though. He could smell their cigarette smoke. If they caught him too far from the camp, they'd beat him bloody.

All he wanted was to go to the bathroom! He sidled around a tree, but the voices in the camp still sounded close.

Bo felt self-conscious, so he took another step into the jungle, then one more. He stepped into the shelter of a high boulder, took care of business—and that's when he saw it.

A banana tree.

A skinny, sickly-looking banana tree, twenty feet uphill from him. Still, three or four of the bananas in the sad-looking bunch looked edible.

Bo risked one step toward the tree, then stopped. If the sentries spotted him, they'd think he was trying to escape. They'd kill him for sure.

Except Teresita needed food for her sisters.

Standing in the shadows, Bo took a shaky breath. He tried to gather his courage, even if there wasn't much there to gather.

Okay. He could do this. He *needed* to do this. With the chatter of the camp behind him, he took a step forward. Then another step, and—

Bo froze.

A dull red dot floated in the darkness higher on the hillside! It was the burning tip of a cigarette.

Which meant a Japanese sentry was standing only twenty feet away, ready to attack any Chamorro who tried to escape.

The glowing ember of cigarette didn't move, though: the sentry hadn't spotted him.

Fear deadened Bo's legs and numbed his fingers. He needed to get the bananas, but the sentry was too close.

Though maybe if he moved slow as a snail, the sentry wouldn't spot him.

Bo held his breath and shifted his weight in the darkness. He felt the soft ground give under his foot. He inhaled slowly, shakily, and—

The red ember in the darkness swayed toward him!

# CHAPTER 10

Stryker raised his hackles warily, but he didn't attack the stranger rushing at Dawson's tent. The stranger was a fellow marine, a skinny human who smelled of canned meat.

Still, Stryker watched carefully just in case.

The marine woke Dawson, then said, "Your dog is staring at me."

"Don't worry about him." Dawson pulled on his boots. "He's just hungry."

The marine stepped back. "What?"

"I'm kidding! I promise Stryker won't go for

your throat." Dawson yawned. "He prefers leg meat."

"Very funny," the marine said. "C'mon, the colonel wants you. Bring the dog."

Dawson attached the patrol collar to Stryker: time to work. The two of them crossed the camp, past foxholes and tents and gun emplacements.

In a big tent, Dawson talked to one of the commanders, older and slower humans who mostly stayed away from the fight. Stryker stood by his side.

"The map you found is important," the commander told Dawson. "Good job, Marine."

"That wasn't me, sir," Dawson said. "It was Stryker."

"He's the marine I was talking to." A faint smile flashed on the older man's craggy face. "Looks like the Japanese are planning to hit us from the peninsula and the jungle at the same time."

"Catching us in the middle," Dawson said.

"One massive charge." The commander nodded. "Trying to knock us off the island. Trying to kill every marine on Guam. We don't expect the

Japanese to attack soon. But when this turns ugly, it'll turn ugly *fast*."

"Yes, sir."

"We need to send a message through enemy territory, to our men on the ridge. Their radios are down, and their lines are cut."

"A written message?"

"That's right, Dawson. But not in English."

Dawson tilted his head, so Stryker tilted his head too. "No?"

"If the Japanese catch our messenger, they might be able to read English. That's why we're going with a backup plan. You've heard of code talkers?"

Dawson shook his head. "Can't say that I have."

"They're Navajo marines who talk to each other in a code based on the Navajo language, giving secret information over the radio. Even if the enemy intercepts the message, they can't understand a word."

"But there's no radio on the ridge . . ."

"Exactly. That's why we're sending a paper message. Still, we'll use code." The man gestured, and a new human stepped forward. "Dawson, this is Carmen Cruz."

The new human was short, with a lot of straight, glossy, black hair. Also, he didn't reek like unwashed clothes and stale sweat. Stryker sniffed more deeply and realized that the new person was *female*! Stryker hadn't met a female human in a long time.

Neither had Dawson. He cleared his throat and said, "Miss."

"Miss Cruz is Chamorro," the old man said.

"Yes, sir." After a pause, Dawson said, "Um, I'm not sure what that means."

"I'm from Guam," the woman explained. "I live here. I was here when the Japanese came, and I'll be here after they're gone."

Her voice was soft—but it was strong. Stryker knew dogs like that; they didn't bark and snarl, but only a fool took their quietness for weakness.

So he wagged at her.

Dawson said, "Stryker likes you. He doesn't usually take to new people."

"He's a beauty," the woman said, holding her hand out for Stryker to sniff.

Stryker already knew what she smelled like, but he was polite enough to sniff anyway.

"There's a radioman on the ridge," the older man told Dawson. "His gear doesn't work, but he's Chamorro too. He'll be able to read the message Miss Cruz writes."

"And none of the Japanese will," the woman said. "If they catch your dog."

Dawson put a hand on Stryker's head, his fingers firm at the base of one of Stryker's ears. He didn't say anything.

"We're sending two messenger dogs," the commander said. "Yours and Ramirez's. They both know Epstein—he's the handler with the men on the ridge. They'll track their way to him, with a little guidance from you?"

"Yes, sir," Dawson said. "If Stryker and Boomer can't do it, it can't be done."

# CHAPTER 11

**W**hen the glow of the sentry's cigarette shifted toward Bo, his nerve broke. All the horrors he'd heard about during the Japanese occupation rose in his memory. All the beatings he'd witnessed appeared again in front of his eyes, and he heard the *crack* of Two Ears's rifle butt against Luis's face.

Keeping his head bowed, Bo scurried back toward the river. The sentry didn't see him, but the fear remained.

He'd failed. He'd tried to be brave—but he'd failed. He slouched back toward the lean-to, slipping past groups of shivering children.

"Bo!" Teresita turned from a farmer she'd been talking to. "What's wrong?"

"Nothing." Bo swallowed. "What're you doing?"

"Trying to find my aunt. She's probably in one of the other camps, though."

"Same with my family, I guess."

"There's no food." Teresita looked toward the main group of Japanese soldiers. "How long are they going to keep us here?"

Bo shrugged. "I don't know. Um, is Luis with your sisters?"

"Uh-huh. The baby is crying, and I . . ." Teresita chewed on her lower lip. "I can't listen to her. She's so hungry and there's nothing to give her. I don't know what to do. I can't—"

"There's a banana tree!" Bo blurted. "I saw a banana tree."

Teresita's face brightened. "Where?"

"Just outside the edge of camp. Past the sentries."

She tucked her hair behind her ears. "Show me."

"I'm not sure that's a good idea." Bo didn't

want to admit he was afraid. "There's a guard in the jungle."

"Just show me!" she said, rising to her full height, which was about an inch shorter than his.

As Bo led her back toward the edge of the camp, he saw a young woman comforting a handful of crying kids.

Teresita squeezed his arm. "Don't look. We need to focus on one thing, okay?"

"O-okay," he said, looking away.

"We'll find the banana tree. One thing."

"Okay."

"We'll grab the bananas. One thing. Then we'll bring them to the kids."

He smiled shakily. "That's three things."

"Ha." She squeezed his arm again. "But only one at a time."

When they reached the edge of the camp, Bo nodded in the direction of the banana tree. "It's in there. How about . . . you stay here and keep watch?"

She snorted. "They're *my* sisters. You stay here. Cough if you see anything."

"Okay," he said, hating the relief that washed over him.

Teresita crept into the woods. A moment before the shadows swallowed her, she looked back over her shoulder. Her eyes were wide with fear, but she gave a little smile and wave.

Then she vanished into the darkness.

Bo scanned for the red glow of a cigarette. He strained his ears for the sound of sentries. Only a few seconds passed, but each one felt like an hour. He exhaled carefully and tried to relax and—there!

He saw motion between the trees. Oh no! Was it soldiers? Was it sentries?

No. It was Teresita! And she had a smile on her face and a handful of bananas in her hands!

He almost called to her. Heck, he almost *laughed*—then he heard boots crunching across the jungle floor, and the jingle of military gear.

Bo's heart stopped beating. He spun toward the soldiers—and saw that one of them was Two Ears.

Behind the soldiers, Teresita froze. The light of

dawn illuminated the fear and horror on her face.

Two Ears and the other soldier turned in her direction. If Bo didn't do something, they'd spot her for sure!

So Bo coughed, as loud as he could.

Except his throat was so dry, that instead of a loud cough, it sounded more like a sigh: *hwoooo.*

And the soldiers didn't hear him! They moved closer to Teresita's hiding place.

"Hey!" Bo heard himself shout in Japanese. "Hey, Two Ears!"

"Who's that?" Two Ears barked, spinning toward him.

"Why do they call you that?" Bo asked, his pulse pounding. "Everyone's got two ears."

Two Ears's face contorted with hatred as he and the other sentry shoved through the jungle. They overlooked Teresita completely . . . and headed right for Bo.

# CHAPTER 12

Dawson attached a pack to Stryker's harness containing medical equipment and ammunition. "Just in case they're running low on supplies."

Stryker twitched his coat, getting used to the weight.

"Run quick, boy," Dawson told Stryker. "Run smart."

Stryker knew his handler was worried about him. He put a paw on Dawson's arm.

Dawson pressed his forehead to Stryker's. "Just come back."

Then he inserted a note into the pouch of the messenger collar, which he strapped around Stryker's neck. Once in this uniform, Stryker ignored everything but Dawson. He'd focus on the message until it was delivered.

He took his place beside Boomer and Ramirez. A quick glance and a deep sniff told Stryker everything he needed to know: Boomer was strong, loyal, and ready.

He was fast too—but not as fast as Stryker.

He let his tongue loll from his mouth, teasing his friend a little, and he heard Boomer shift beside him. He was carrying his own message and getting ready to run—to try to beat Stryker.

The humans led them along the paths that ran closer to the battlefront. A grenade exploded in the jungle far ahead, and a scream ripped through the dawn. Rifle fire cracked and cracked again. There was a gasp and a *boom*.

Stryker felt his hackles rise as they moved closer to the battle. Closer to the sharp jaws of war.

Medics passed them from farther along the path, carrying injured marines on stretchers toward the distant hospital. Stryker followed

Dawson off the path, through filthy, muddy trenches that stank of blood and worse.

After a short time, they reached what the humans called "the front." It was a ragged boundary that ran through the jungle at the base of a hill, dotted with trenches and foxholes. As they got closer, the noise turned thunderous, deafening. Men shouted, and Dawson almost had to crawl to avoid getting shot.

Staying low, Dawson led Stryker toward the leafy crown of a fallen tree.

"Report!" Dawson told Stryker. "Report to Epstein."

Stryker knew Epstein. He knew his scent. They'd trained together, Epstein and Dawson and Ramirez, alongside Boomer and Stryker. Those three humans were the most important landmarks in Stryker's mind. He'd learned to race from one to another, bringing supplies or messages. Now when the marines needed a quick, strong warrior to travel through dangerous territory, they sent a war dog from one trainer to another.

Ramirez told the same to Boomer, and the dogs started running.

Stryker zigged one direction, Boomer zagged the other.

Keeping low.

Running fast.

A sniper's bullet whined past Stryker's ear. He heard the *chunk* of impact behind him.

He was afraid for Dawson, but he kept running. Keeping to the underbrush. Trying to stay covered, trying to stay ahead of the enemy, though he sensed them all around.

The Japanese were charging. Dozens of soldiers, maybe hundreds, poured out of trenches and jungle barricades. They fired wildly and swarmed toward the American foxholes on the front.

Answering fire dropped them—but not quickly enough. The Japanese attackers kept screaming, they kept advancing!

Stryker zigged and zagged until he was out of range of the gunfire.

He was about to spin around—to return to his mission—when he heard something. Two men were fighting in a foxhole nearby. One carried the familiar smells of Stryker's marine camp. The other didn't.

Stryker zigged again, pricking his ears to track the sound. A bullet nicked the bag strapped to his shoulder, tugging him sideways, but he didn't slow.

A member of his pack was in trouble!

He launched himself into a foxhole and landed on the back of a Japanese soldier. The enemy had been standing over a marine with a bleeding arm, about to stab him with a bayonet like a long fang.

The Japanese soldier stumbled when Stryker hit him, shouting in surprise.

Stryker slammed into the wall of the foxhole, panting and dizzy. He tumbled to the muddy ground. Before he could scramble to his paws, the enemy soldier loomed over him.

# CHAPTER 13

Two Ears's bayonet glinted in the dim dawn light as he stomped toward Bo. His boots crushed twigs and splashed in mud.

The murder in his eyes terrified Bo. He was about to die. He was going to die right here in this muddy patch of jungle.

Then a quick cough cut through the patter of rain. It was Teresita!

The soldiers paused for a heartbeat. They glanced over their shoulders before refocusing on Bo.

But that tiny pause was enough to save Bo's life.

He took off running. Leaves slapped his face, and branches snagged his arms. His feet splashed in mud as he tripped over roots and rocks.

He heard Two Ears close behind him, swearing and slashing with his bayonet.

Bo slipped on a slimy patch of leaves. He hit the ground hard, rolled onto his hands and feet—then stopped.

He could hear Two Ears shouldering through a thicket a few feet away. Frozen in terror, Bo waited for the shout—or the bayonet—but nothing happened.

Two Ears couldn't see him in the dark shadows. Instead, the soldier lifted his head and scanned the jungle.

A voice from lower on the hill shouted in Japanese, "Did you catch him?"

"Not yet," Two Ears answered. "But I will."

Bo shivered at the words, then crawled slowly away. His pulse spiked at the sound of every crinkling leaf and snapping twig. The fear made him dizzy, but he kept going until he reached a clearing overlooking the overcrowded Chamorro camp.

He blinked at the sight in front of him. A half-dozen Japanese soldiers stood around a tall object covered in waterproof canvas. They hadn't noticed him. They weren't even looking in his direction.

". . . the Americans are still advancing," one said in a low voice.

Another grunted. "We'll stop them on the coast."

"As long as they don't get any help from the natives." A third soldier rested a hand on the tall object. "And they won't. We've got them surrounded by *these* . . ."

Careful not to move too fast, Bo wiped mud and water from his eyes. He looked more closely at the object, and his blood chilled.

It was a machine gun.

The Chamorros in the valley camp were surrounded by machine guns because the Japanese were worried that they'd join forces with the Americans.

Which meant the Japanese would massacre the

Chamorros to keep them from fighting. They'd kill them all, from the oldest grandmother to the youngest baby.

Crouched there in the darkness, Bo felt cold, hungry, and terrified. But despite his fear, for once he knew exactly what he needed to do. And he knew he wouldn't hesitate, no matter how scared he got.

He needed to sneak through the jungle *toward* the battle. Toward the sound of the guns and shells.

He needed to tell the Americans what was happening.

# CHAPTER 14

**S**tryker struggled to his paws. He bared his teeth and snarled—but the Japanese soldier in the foxhole swung his rifle like a club.

An instant before the blow landed, the marine with the bleeding arm jabbed the enemy from behind with a shovel.

Then he slammed the soldier's knee with the metal blade.

With an angry snarl, the Japanese soldier tried to point his rifle at the marine, but his knee buckled. The marine pulled him into a scuffle on the muddy ground. The fight was ugly, breathless, and desperate.

And it was over in a moment.

The marine winced at his wounded arm. He'd lost his helmet during the fight, and his light hair surprised Stryker. A strange color for a coat.

"You okay?" the man asked, looking at Stryker.

Stryker shook himself. His legs felt strong and his ears sharp.

"Of course you are. You're a marine."

Stryker licked the man's bleeding arm. You need to lick wounds so they heal. Everyone knew that—except humans.

"Get off me, pup," the light-haired marine said, pushing Stryker away—and giving him a pat at the same time. "This is no time for kissing."

Stryker licked him again.

The man snorted and pushed himself to his feet. "Okay, pup. We're not done yet."

The battle wasn't over. Stryker waited for a break in the gunfire. He needed to deliver his message. He climbed to the edge of the foxhole, digging his claws into the sloping earth. He could hear the crunch of debris beneath enemy boots.

They were stalking closer to the foxhole.

Stryker pointed his snout in the direction of the threat, going perfectly still.

The light-haired marine glanced at him. "You sure about that, pup?"

Stryker didn't move a muscle.

The man took a breath—then in one motion he straightened and fired. The *crack* of the shot stung Stryker's ears, but he still heard the enemy soldier fall.

The marine grunted in satisfaction. "We have to get out of this foxhole. We're out here on our lonesome. I don't know what your excuse is. I got separated from my—"

Stryker ignored him and listened to the sounds of the enemy gathering. He needed to find Epstein and complete his mission. He scrambled onto the battlefield, zigzagging through clouds of smoke. The smell pricked at his nose.

Behind him, he heard the light-haired man climb from the foxhole and start running just before a grenade exploded, throwing dirt and rocks everywhere.

The light-haired marine raced for cover. Stryker

ran in the other direction. He needed to keep moving until he smelled Epstein.

He flashed through the jungle and burst into a clearing. Not the safest place to be. He needed to—

The earth spat at him! Machine gun fire was tracking toward him!

Stryker leaped and turned in the air. He landed and launched himself forward, faster than any human. Faster than any of the other war dogs—speeding closer and closer to the safety of the underbrush.

He couldn't outrun a machine gun. The bullets tore into the earth behind him. He knew that the next ones would strike him before he reached cover.

Still, he was a marine. He never gave up. He just ran faster: loyal to his mission, to his handler, to his pack.

Enemy rounds burned through the air directly at Stryker.

They hit their target!

But they didn't hit *Stryker*. Instead, a yelp

sounded from the rear as Stryker dove into the underbrush.

That was Boomer's yelp!

And that was Boomer's scent.

When Stryker glanced over his shoulder, he saw Boomer lying bleeding on the ground in the clearing. He'd leaped in front of the bullets aimed for Stryker. He'd saved his life . . . and saved the mission.

As Stryker watched, Boomer's tail wagged one final time. Then his eyes fluttered closed.

# CHAPTER 15

Two Ears stepped closer to Bo, his uniform a dark shape in the dawn light of the jungle. His boot landed in the mud three feet from Bo's hand.

Bo didn't whimper. He didn't flinch. He didn't even breathe.

And in a moment, Two Ears continued past. Only a few steps, but enough so that Bo's heart started beating again.

The soldiers around the machine gun laughed.

Two Ears took another few steps, scanning the jungle.

Bo squeezed his eyes tight. He prayed to God for protection. He thought of his mother and father, who were somewhere on the island, probably thinking of him. He also thought of his sister, who was quiet and shy but as stubborn as a boulder.

Then he started crawling.

The leaves rustled loudly under his knees, yet somehow Two Ears didn't appear from the darkness. A trickle of muddy water soaked Bo's neck as he crawled blindly uphill, trying to get away from the Japanese soldiers.

Bo left the voices behind. He wormed through what felt like an endless field of ferns. Eventually he reached a leaf-strewn forest floor dotted with boulders.

After he'd crawled for half an hour . . . he kept crawling. Because every time he thought of rising to his feet, he remembered the look on Two Ears's face.

Eventually, exhaustion hit. Bo slumped against a boulder and caught his breath. The yellow dawn light streamed through the trees, warming the damp leaves and soil and raising a thin mist.

Bo inhaled. The rich, earthy scent of the jungle was comforting . . . but it made him hungry.

A few birds chirped, and Bo realized that he couldn't hear the sound of battle anymore.

*Must be a lull in the fighting,* he thought. That was okay, he knew he needed to head west and north.

He rubbed the ache from his neck. He needed to get moving, to put some distance between himself and the camp by morning. He needed to—

The birds fell silent, and his breath caught.

Something must've spooked them.

Something nearby.

Bo tilted his head, listening. He heard nothing, nothing . . . then a soft crunching. Followed by the crack of twigs, the crumple of leaves.

The chill seeped back into Bo's bones: Two Ears had tracked him!

Bo didn't know if he should flee or hide. He didn't know if he was already in the sights of Two Ears's rifle. He took a breath and—

A deep grunting came from the gloom.

Then a guttural, animal snorting.

"Oh, no," Bo muttered.

That wasn't Two Ears . . . it was a wild boar!

In a flash, Bo scrambled to his feet. A snouty grunt sent him galloping in the other direction. A boar would gore him with its tusks if it was scared or mad.

Bo fled through the jungle, grabbing thick stalks to pull himself along. His feet slapped the ground, and the drizzle speckled his face. He ran and ran, his lungs aching and his legs pounding.

At the base of a gnarled tree, he put his hands on his knees to catch his breath. When his panting stopped, he listened for the boar. He didn't hear a single snort. Thank God.

Wait.

*There.*

Was someone talking? Yes! Someone was cursing in Japanese.

Bo almost broke down. That was Two Ears!

He must've heard Bo's wild flight from the boar. Now he was swearing in rage, his voice slashing through a sudden torrent of rain.

Hunting for Bo.

# CHAPTER 16

The drizzle turned into a downpour that drenched Stryker. Rivulets snaked down the jungle hillside, joining into fast, muddy streams.

With gunfire still sounding behind him, Stryker trotted forward. He'd caught Epstein's scent on the battlefield, then lost it again in the rain.

He knew it was coming from above, though— from the top of a hill or the peak of a jungle ridge. His paws ached, a scratch on his side itched, and the rain-soaked pack on his back felt heavy and awkward.

Still, Stryker remembered that last wag of Boomer's tail and didn't let himself slow down. He'd find Epstein—for his pack, and for Boomer.

The rainstorm muffled his hearing. The world smelled of mud and water. He couldn't see much through the downpour.

He turned uphill, followed a tumbling stream through the jungle—then paused. Japanese soldiers! Not too close, but not too far either.

They were hidden in a pillbox—a concrete mound—on the hillside. Or lying in ambush.

Stryker wasn't patrolling. There was nobody to warn and nobody to protect. He needed to deliver his message to Epstein, that was all. So he looped around the Japanese, heading higher on the hillside. He climbed a slope, loped between dripping bushes and—

Pain!

A stab of pain in his hip!

He staggered before he even heard the gunshot, a dull *thuck* in the rainstorm. A bullet hole thudded into a tree trunk a foot from his ear! A sniper was firing at him!

He needed to make a break for it. He needed to *run*.

Another bullet shook the bush Stryker was under, and he burst out. He ignored the pain in his hip and raced forward. He veered to the left— then to the right.

Bullets slammed into roots and pinged off rocks.

Stryker leaped over a fallen tree and almost lost his footing because of his injured leg. He flashed along a shallow jungle ravine and found himself in a gap between the trees.

Another bullet whistled overhead, and Stryker ran. Faster and faster uphill.

The pain in his hip flared when he veered to the right. He almost yelped, but he'd been trained to stay silent. He stumbled again and scrambled in the soggy leaves before racing higher.

After his frantic flight, Stryker found himself on the peak of a ridge, peering out across the green jungle. It looked almost peaceful, with the mist covering the chaos and destruction. The treetops swayed in the rain beneath the gray clouds. A

torrent of water roared below him.

He crept to the edge of the ridge and inhaled deeply, trying to detect a hint of Epstein. Or of any marines. He couldn't smell anything except the damp vegetation of the jungle and—

A mortar exploded on the other side of a tree. Debris pelted Stryker's side, and the shock wave shoved him off the ridge.

He hurtled through the air.

When he hit the ground, pain burst in his wounded hip. He rolled over and over—then *splash!*

Water filled his mouth and soaked his coat, dragging him downward. He'd fallen into a river, but he was too weak to swim! He struggled to keep his nose above the surface as the current carried him away.

# CHAPTER 17

The rainstorm plastered Bo's hair to his head and chilled him through his clothes. The jungle was hot when the sun was high, but it was still early morning and Bo was soaked to the skin. As he listened to Two Ears cursing, he spun to his left, then desperately to his right.

He didn't know which way to run!

Uphill. He'd head uphill and away from—

A sudden thought stopped him. Why was Two Ears cursing so *loudly*?

The guttural snorting came a second later, a rough, piggish grunt. Wait—was the boar attacking Two Ears?

Bo almost laughed. Judging from the sound, at the very least the boar was scaring Two Ears. Terrifying him.

Time to run.

Despite his wobbly legs, Bo raced away from the boulder. Branches stabbed him, but he didn't care; in the rain Two Ears couldn't hear him, couldn't track him. Especially while facing an angry boar.

Still, Bo didn't slow. He ran until he couldn't run another step—then he kept running.

The sound of battle grumbled through the lashing rain. The noise was soft, coming from across the island. Grenades, tanks, artillery. Every now and then the wind brought the *tik-tik-tik* of machine gun fire—but from far ahead of him, thank God.

Not from behind him.

Not from the encampment.

Bo stumbled when the crack of a rifle came

from closer than the other sounds. Maybe it was Two Ears, maybe it wasn't. Maybe someone was aiming for Bo, maybe for the boar.

He didn't care. He didn't stop. He needed to find the Americans, that's all that mattered.

The rain slowed. The shelling intensified. Lizards fled at his crashing, panting approach.

Bo jogged mindlessly through the brush until the jungle blurred around him. His imagination drifted back to a happier time. Into the warmth of his childhood, years ago, before the Japanese invasion.

He remembered watching his cousins tend a corn field, guiding huge carabao pulling metal plows. The animals had looked like shaggy monsters to Bo's young eyes, but they were gentle.

His parents weren't farmers, but they worked the fields because of *adalalak*: the Chamorro tradition of helping relatives and neighbors.

Which had made sense to young Bo. "I can help too!" he'd said.

"You stay out of the way," his sister told him, ruffling his hair fondly.

The next thing he remembered was his parents

and sister repairing their home's roof after a storm. His sister was eight years older than Bo, and got to do all the good stuff, like climb on the roof.

Bo wanted to be up there too. He'd been about to ask when he'd heard sailors' voices outside. He'd run to the door to peek at the pale American sailors in their funny costumes. A few hundred of them lived on the naval base, but Bo hadn't seen them often.

One of the sailors threw him a candy. "Here, kid."

*"Dangkulu na si Yu'us ma'ase!"* Bo sang out. Which meant *thank you very much.*

"Dang-a-lang a ding-dong to you, too!" the sailor said, and tossed him another candy.

Bo returned inside, smiling happily. But to his surprise, his father was frowning at what he'd overheard.

"What's wrong?" Bo asked.

His father told him that the US Navy had occupied Guam for more than forty years. The entire island had been designated as a naval base without ever asking what the people who lived there wanted. "We don't even choose our own leader," his father said. "We're ruled by the navy governor."

"He seems nice," Bo said.

"That's true," Bo's mother said. "But it doesn't matter. This is our land. Our people lived here for thousands of years. We should choose."

Bo had heard this conversation before. His parents didn't like that the Chamorros needed to follow navy rules and they couldn't even vote. The navy just took what they wanted. If you didn't like it, too bad.

Of course the navy had treated the people better than the Japanese soldiers, who forced the Chamorros to feed them and work for them— using beatings and worse as punishment.

Still, Bo hoped that after the war, the American military would give the Chamorros more rights and stop taking their land.

Bo's mother hadn't let him eat his candy until after dinner. First, he'd stuffed himself with *kadon guihan*, fish stew, then popped one of the sweets into his mouth.

And now, staggering through the jungle in a stupor, he remembered the burst of flavor on his tongue. He remembered the feeling of fullness from dinner. He remembered the sense of safety, knowing that his parents and sister were there for him.

They'd always been there for him when he was a little kid, but they couldn't help him now. Nobody could help him now—and nobody could help the people in the encampment *except* for him.

So despite his fear and exhaustion, and the pounding ache in his feet, Bo kept running. When his legs threatened to give out, he slowed to a walk. When he couldn't walk anymore, he shambled onward. He didn't know where he was going, except westward. Toward the battle. Toward the Americans.

He needed to tell them about those machine guns threatening thousands of people. Of course, he didn't even know *which* Americans to tell, and he didn't know how he'd convince them. That didn't matter right now.

He focused on one thing: he kept staggering onward, dizzy and weak.

At least until he reached the river.

Then he knelt down to take a drink . . . and collapsed.

He couldn't go on any longer. He couldn't force himself to his feet—and he'd never felt so alone.

# CHAPTER 18

The river current soaked into Stryker's fur and backpack, weighing him down. He paddled his paws, struggling to keep his muzzle above water.

He tried to swim to the sodden banks of the river, but his legs turned numb and useless. He couldn't smell anything with water splashing into his nose. The only sound he heard was the smack of the river against his ears.

He sank under the surface.

He choked and gasped. Summoning his

strength, he paddled harder and thrust his snout above the waterline. He sucked in a lungful of air. He drifted weakly, spinning and dizzy, battered by floating debris.

He was fading. He'd never deliver the message.

He'd never smell Dawson again.

Dawson.

The thought of his human gave him a final spark of strength. When the muddy bottom of the river snagged his paws, Stryker half swam and half clawed himself toward the bank.

At least he tried. But the current was too strong. Stryker couldn't pull himself out of the water.

Exhaustion seeped into his bones. His eyes closed. He sank beneath the surface again and—

Something grabbed him!

Teeth clamped onto the strap of his pack and pulled.

Stryker's eyes feebly cracked open and he saw a human. Those weren't teeth, they were *hands*. A young human tugged at Stryker, his legs splashing into the water, his feet sinking into the mud.

"C'mon, you dumb dog!" the young human moaned, slipping down the bank. "Help me out! I can barely stand, I can't do this alone."

The silly child was going to fall into the river! Stryker couldn't let that happen. Summoning the last of his strength, he paddled furiously as the boy heaved him toward the water's edge.

"C'mon, c'mon," the boy groaned.

Giving one mighty pull, the boy flopped backward onto the riverbank, yanking Stryker from the water—and onto the boy's narrow chest.

For a moment they lay there panting, with the boy's feet in the water and Stryker on top of him. Then the boy wrapped his arms around Stryker and started crying.

Stryker licked his face.

"Ew," the boy said, and hugged him tighter.

Stryker licked him again.

"You're warm," the boy said. "And stinky."

They remained there in a dripping embrace until the boy regained his strength. He rolled to the side, gently laying Stryker on the riverbank.

"Where'd you come from? What are you *wearing*?" The boy picked at the backpack . . .

then froze. "You—you're wounded!"

Stryker shook water from his eyes.

"You are too!" the boy said. "You're bleeding and—oh! You're carrying gear. You're an American fighting dog! There's bandages and . . ."

Stryker lifted his head when the boy's voice trailed off.

"Is this *food*?" The boy made a noise like a puppy curling up for a nap. "What are Ration D Bars? Tropical bars?"

The boy rummaged in the pack. Stryker smelled human food, sickly sweet and unnatural. He licked his injured leg and listened to the boy taking a bite.

"Yech. That's disgusting," the boy said. "And the best thing I've ever eaten. Here."

Stryker sniffed the square of food, then turned away.

"You don't want? More for me, then." The boy finished the rations and looked at Stryker. "So, you're with the US Marines? That means you know where they are."

The boy sounded nervous, so Stryker gave his stubby tail a reassuring wag.

"Good!" The boy stroked Stryker's back. "Good dog. I need to find them. I need to tell them something. Except I don't know if they'll believe me." The boy fell silent for a second. "Well, I still have to try. Can you get up?"

The boy touched Stryker's belly and gently patted his chest, so Stryker stood and shook himself thoroughly.

"Gee, thanks," the boy said. "I wasn't wet *enough*."

Stryker tested his leg. Not strong enough to hold all his weight, but not weak enough to keep him from walking.

"Go home, boy!" the human child said. "Go home to the marines!"

Stryker knew the word "home." He twitched his ears and sniffed. The boy smelled desperate and exhausted.

This human *definitely* needed home. That made sense. Stryker knew how he felt.

Stryker couldn't continue his mission right now either. Not after being hurt and almost drowned. Being out of the water was helping, but he needed more time to recover.

So he took a few limping steps, then looked over his shoulder to tell the boy to follow.

"I'm coming, I'm coming," the boy said, licking his fingers. "You're a smart one, aren't you? Are we going home? Good boy!"

Stryker limped downhill until he found a marshy spot to cross the river. After coming so close to drowning, he still felt wary of the water. He paused there to gather his strength.

"Come on," the boy said, stepping into the water. "Is this the way home? Go home! Home to the marines!"

Stryker didn't come—the boy was too young to obey—but he waited for the boy to splash back to him.

"Here." The boy unstrapped the pack from Stryker's back. "I'll hold this."

Stryker eyed him before deciding that was okay. As long as the boy didn't try to take his message collar.

He limped into the marsh. The boy followed, wading through the muck. The rotten-egg stink filled Stryker's nostrils and the mud coated his legs and clung to his belly fur.

The boy grumbled and whined as the sun moved through the sky overhead. Poor humans. They were good at reaching things in high branches, but other than that they couldn't manage much by themselves.

On the other side of the marsh, Stryker headed for higher, drier ground.

"Is this the way home?" the boy asked. "Home? We're going home?"

Stryker sniffed the air, and a faint thread of scent caught his attention. It smelled like home to him, dry and safe. He started through the jungle, walking mostly on three legs and keeping the wounded fourth leg curled under as blood matted his fur. The sun was getting lower and it was time to find shelter.

Still, he made better time than the boy, who could barely even lift his two legs. He shuffled and stumbled, so Stryker kept waiting for him to catch up.

Then the boy stopped at a tree with fat, jagged leaves. "Hey! Wait up! This is breadfruit!"

Stryker didn't bother pausing. He just glanced back for a moment.

"Come back!" The boy grabbed a heavy green pod from the ground. "Come back, you dumb dog!"

Stryker sniffed the breeze. Not far now. Soon they'd reach *home*.

When he heard the boy shuffling closer, he started off again. The boy muttered behind him, but Stryker didn't let it bother him. Humans liked to make noises.

"Are we there? Just over that ridge? Is that home?"

Stryker wagged encouragingly at the word "home," then followed the scent around a rocky rise between jungle trees.

He limped down the other side—and waited. He heard the boy's uneven shuffle through the leaves. He smelled the boy's fatigue.

Stryker didn't feel much better. His hip and leg flared with pain, and he was only walking on three paws. They couldn't go farther without rest. Luckily, they didn't need to.

When the boy approached, Stryker hobbled into the dry patch beneath the boulders.

"Go home!" the boy said, staggering closer.

Stryker lowered himself to the ground, careful of his wound.

"This isn't home, boy. Go *home*."

Stryker wagged once, to show that he accepted the boy's gratitude for finding them a dry den—a safe home for the evening. As safe as possible, with a war raging outside.

# CHAPTER 19

**B**o almost wept at the sight in front of him. This wasn't home! This wasn't the American military. This wasn't anything that could help the thousands of scared, hungry Chamorros being held prisoner in that encampment.

Instead, a couple of mossy boulders loomed behind a ferny patch of hillside. And the dog waited inside the wide, protected space between the rocks. But it wasn't *that* wide. Not even wide enough for Bo to stretch his arms. And only five or six feet high.

Still, the dog wriggled aside to give Bo room to enter.

"Dumb dog," he repeated. "This isn't home."

The dog's ears drooped, and for a second Bo felt bad for calling him dumb. Then the dog started licking at the slash across the top of one leg. Poor guy. That cut looked like it hurt.

Bo crouched and scooted out of the rain. The space between the boulders was deeper than it looked. Drier too. And carpeted with fallen leaves. It was actually a pretty cozy nook, though it stank of wet dog—and swampy boy.

Bo slumped against the rock wall. He couldn't stop here, not for long. Still, he needed to rest for a few minutes or he'd collapse.

"Okay," he told the dog. "We'll stay here until we warm up."

The dog stopped licking his cut and looked at Bo.

"What's your name?" Bo asked, setting aside the breadfruit and the pack.

The dog eyed the breadfruit, his wet ears twitching.

"Oh, you want some *lemmai?*" Bo asked.

"Maybe that's your name? Is your name Lemmai?"

The dog's tongue lolled from his very toothy mouth.

"Of course I'll share, Lemmai. After all, you gave me those tropical bars."

On his fourth try, Bo tore through the tough outer skin of the breadfruit. The fruit was soft and ripe—but nobody ate breadfruit raw. The inside looked gummy and gross. Bo's mom always baked or roasted it. Still, he figured it was better than nothing.

He gave the dog half the fruit and took a bite of the other half. Yech. Well, maybe the dog had some more of those rations.

Bo dug through the pack and found medical stuff. Safety pins, gauze bandages, scissors, tape, ointment. Iodine swabs. Hmm. He read the directions on the ointment, then looked at the dog's wounded leg.

"If I clean your cut, are you going to bite me?"

The dog tore into the fruit with wolflike fangs.

"Oh, good," Bo said. "That's reassuring."

Still, he took a breath and scooted closer. The wet-dog stink almost made his eyes water. He touched the dog's unhurt side, then carefully parted the dog's fur around the injury.

The dog stopped eating and watched him with alert eyes.

"I'm trying to help you, Lemmai. Okay?" The cut looked more like a burn than a stab, and Bo guessed that a bullet had grazed the dog. "Whoa. You got shot and you kept swimming?"

The dog lowered his head again and chomped on the raw breadfruit.

"Here goes," Bo said, and applied the ointment to the wound.

The dog flinched, then tensed his muscles. Bo spoke softly to him, trying to keep him calm and coat the entire wound. But he was tired and shaky; his hand slipped and he jabbed the cut with his thumbnail.

The dog yelped and whipped around toward him.

"Sorry!" Bo said.

The dog thrust his muzzle at Bo's throat—

then licked his face.

Bo laughed. "You know I'm helping, don't you, Lemmai?"

The dog licked him again.

"Gah. You smell like a wet carabao."

Bo finished smearing on the ointment. He looked at the bandages but couldn't figure how to apply them to a dog. He checked another pocket of the pack and found scissors, a compass, and a lighter.

A *lighter*!

Bo couldn't remember the last time he'd been warm and dry. While the dog chomped on breadfruit, he peeled away the bark from some branches to get at the drier wood beneath. Then he stacked the branches inside a small circle of stones, but even the driest kindling he could find was too damp to build a fire. The most he could do was create a thin pillar of smoke that rose above Bo and the dog, into a natural chimney between the boulders.

Bo reached for his breadfruit, and it was gone.

The dog had eaten both halves.

"Lemmai! You jerk!"

The dog wagged his tiny tail and snuggled closer.

Bo stroked the dog's head and flopped his ears. "Greedy carabao. Well, I'll grab more fruit when we leave. And we *are* leaving. Any minute now."

The dog put his muzzle on Bo's leg and seemed to smile up at him. Bo scratched the wet fur on the dog's neck. The dog closed his eyes sleepily, enjoying the attention.

Bo smiled. As he huddled closer to the dog for warmth, he found himself telling the dog everything. He told him about life on the island for the past few years, living with the constant fear of the Japanese. Then about last week, being separated from his family and forced to clear trails in the jungle. Then about the march to the encampment and his escape from Two Ears.

Talking about it helped, for some reason. Bo wasn't alone anymore. He wasn't *afraid* anymore. He wasn't even *awake* anymore.

He drifted into sleep, dreaming of a world without bombs, without guns. Without an angry soldier hunting him through the jungle . . .

# CHAPTER 20

**B**o awoke with a jerk.

Hazy dawn light seeped into the little cave. He didn't feel rested, but he must've slept for a few hours.

Lemmai was snuggled beside him, fast asleep. Poor dog. Bo couldn't imagine how tired he was. He patted the dog softly and noticed that his filthy collar was weird. Thick and oversized.

It was another pouch.

Maybe there were more tropical bars inside!

Bo kept patting Lemmai as he opened the

collar pouch. He didn't find food, though. Instead, he found a tube. And inside that tube, there was a rolled-up note.

Weird.

Bo couldn't read the message in the dim light, so he crawled from the cave.

The rain had stopped, and sunlight glimmered through the cloudy sky. Bo stretched and started toward the breadfruit tree.

He scanned the jungle for tastier food—bananas or coconuts—as the sunlight brightened through the clouds. He walked a little farther into a patch of sunshine, then stopped to read the note.

It wasn't in English.

It was in Chamorro!

Some of it didn't make sense. The Chamorro words seemed to have unusual meanings. But Bo *thought* it said: "Scouts found a map. Enemy gathering. Planning a timed attack from the peninsula and eastern front." Then a bunch of numbers. "Prepare to repel from both sides."

That was pretty close, at least. All Bo knew for sure was that the message contained military orders in Chamorro. Which was weird. Why write an American message in Chamorro?

"Oh!" Bo said.

Lemmai was a military dog, sent through enemy lines. They must have written in Chamorro as a code! Lemmai must have been delivering this message when he'd been shot!

Then Bo realized there was something even odder about the writing.

He *recognized* it.

The handwriting was familiar. *Very* familiar.

It was his sister's. He was sure of it. His sister had written this code. But that didn't make any sense. What was *she* doing with the US military?

He grinned. *Who cares? She's alive!*

And Bo only needed to follow Lemmai to find her! Plus, she'd know exactly which American to warn about the machine guns surrounding the camp.

Bo squared his shoulders.

Nothing could stop him now.

Nothing could—

"You!" Two Ears spat, grabbing Bo's arm.

The jungle spun.

The sunlight dimmed.

Bo felt like he'd been swallowed up in a nightmare.

How had Two Ears found him? This couldn't be happening!

Mud streaked the Japanese soldier's face and pants. His uniform was torn and tattered and blood seeped through his pant leg.

Two Ears clamped his hand hard around Bo's neck. "Stupid runt."

"I'm not the one who wrestled a pig."

Two Ears slapped him twice. When Bo fell to his knees, Two Ears tore the message from his hand.

"What's this? This isn't English. Are you writing notes to your mommy?"

"Yeah," Bo said, cupping his bloody nose.

Two Ears ripped the note into tiny pieces that fluttered when he threw them. "You're not going to see her again."

He took a handful of Bo's shirt in his hand and lifted him to his feet.

Instead of begging for his life, Bo struggled. He tried to kick Two Ears, he tried to bite—but the Japanese soldier was too strong. He'd lost his rifle and his hat, but not his strength.

Not his rage.

He slammed Bo to the ground and pulled his arm sideways. "This is what happens to runts."

A cold pit opened in Bo's stomach. As Two Ears started dragging him into the jungle, Bo could only think to do one thing. He took a deep breath and screamed for Lemmai.

# CHAPTER 21

When Stryker woke in the cave, the boy was gone. He flattened his ears unhappily. He'd slept as deeply as a newborn puppy! Being injured and exhausted was no excuse. He'd slept deeper than was safe.

Not even the boy's departure had awoken him.

Stryker pointed his snout toward the fresh air. He smelled nothing except the stench of wet wood smoke. He raised his ears. Leaves shivered in the jungle outside, trickles of water dropped, and distant gunfire sounded.

But he didn't sense the boy.

He sniffed at his wounded hip. He curled his lip at the disgusting medicinal stench. Humans didn't lick with their tongues, they licked with their fingers. And the boy had coated his cut with a special spit that was bitter and goopy.

Stryker didn't like the smell, but he'd been trained to accept it.

When he stood, his leg felt better. The pain still stabbed into him, but his muscles felt stronger. Maybe just from sleeping off his exhaustion for a few hours.

He shook himself, then smelled a smear of fruit on the floor. Much better than the bitter mineral stink of the medicine! He licked the ground, and—

There! A noise from outside.

A deep, angry voice.

Before he even realized what he'd heard, Stryker burst from the cave. His wounded leg burned, but he didn't let it slow him down. He flashed through the undergrowth, a dark blur in the shadows.

Fast. Focused. Hunting his prey.

Protecting his boy.

Stryker burst from the trees.

In a single heartbeat, he saw the enemy soldier dragging the boy into the jungle.

The boy screamed.

Without hesitation, Stryker launched himself at the man's arm, his teeth clamping tight before either human realized he was there. Dobermans like Stryker had strong jaws, and he'd been trained to never let go.

The man howled and spun, whirling Stryker in a circle, trying to dislodge him.

Stryker bit down harder, and the man slammed him against a tree trunk.

The wound in his side flared.

Agony washed through him.

The man hit him against the tree again.

Stryker felt himself weakening, and the boy— that skinny, hairless puppy—dove closer and grabbed the man's calves in a tight hug.

The enemy fell to the ground, smashing down hard among the leaves and rocks.

Stryker fell too—but not for long.

Ignoring the pain in his leg, he regained his

feet. The boy stood beside him, holding a small rock in one of his trembling, clawless fists.

The enemy rose high above them. He smelled shaken but enraged. He was a big animal—bigger than Stryker and the boy combined.

He took a step toward them.

Stryker growled deep in his throat and showed his teeth.

The enemy raised his hand, threatening the boy.

The boy didn't flinch. He remained strong, standing beside Stryker. Stryker heard the boy's heart pounding furiously . . . but his furless feet stayed planted and his rock stayed ready.

The boy stank of mud and fear—but beneath the fear, Stryker sensed determination. He sensed a bond. His boy would stay beside him. They'd fight together, win or lose.

The enemy took another step forward.

The boy told the man, "Y-you better get out of here."

Stryker didn't understand the words, but he knew a threat when he heard one. The boy's voice shook, yet his hand remained steady.

Stryker stalked forward a single step, and the boy matched him.

The enemy didn't look away from Stryker. He watched his snarling muzzle and his tensed shoulders. Stryker bared his teeth wider and growled. Another threat, a deadly one.

Not even a Doberman could beat a gun, but this man didn't have a gun. He didn't have fur or claws or teeth. He didn't even have a *pack*. He was big and strong, but weaponless and alone.

Stryker took another step forward.

Again, the boy matched him.

Stryker smelled the sweat on the man's forehead. He heard the man's pulse beating. Fat raindrops trickled off the trees overhead and speckled the leaves.

Stryker heard them fall and stared at the man's throat.

"I'll get my gun," the man snarled at the boy. "I'll kill you both."

The rage in the man's voice made Stryker's hackles rise.

The boy must've heard the same thing. Stryker smelled his fear turn to anger and his anger turn to determination. Good. Determination mattered more than courage.

"First I'll shoot your dog," the man ranted. "And then—"

"No, you won't," the boy said, and hurled his rock at the man's chest.

Stryker was already in motion, springing forward.

The rock struck the enemy. The man staggered, and Stryker clamped onto his arm with his jaws . . . and this time he didn't hold back.

The man howled in agony. Stryker released his arm, and the man fled into the jungle, stumbling over rocks.

"I'm smiling now!" the boy shouted after him, his voice hoarse. "I'm smiling at you!"

When the sound of the man faded, Stryker looked at the boy, so he'd know they were safe.

The boy dropped to his knees and gave Stryker a very unmilitary hug. He wept and squeezed Stryker. He even kissed his snout once or twice or ten times. Stryker wagged enthusiastically—to help pack morale. A good war dog supported his humans.

But Stryker needed to get on with the mission.

"Let's get moving," the boy finally said, wiping tears from his face. "We've got to deliver your message."

Stryker sniffed out a half-rotten fruit on the ground and started eating.

"We'll find my sister, and I'll tell her about the machine guns. She'll know what to do."

Stryker kept eating.

"Except . . ." The boy frowned at the ground. "The message is gone."

He rummaged among the leaves. When he picked up a tiny scrap of damp paper, Stryker sniffed it helpfully. It wasn't edible, though. Silly human.

"I can't even read the bits that are left. I guess I remember the words, though. And all those numbers. I'll just tell them. Except . . . do you even know where the Americans are?"

Stryker finished the fruit and peed on a tree. That way, if the wounded enemy soldier came back, he'd know he was crossing the line.

"Oh, thanks," the boy said. "That's helpful. If I tell you to go home, you'll just lead me to another cave. Um. What's the right command? Deliver! *Deliver*, boy?"

Stryker peed on another tree, because you couldn't be too careful.

"Message! Um, *carry*! Um . . . Bring the—the message—" The boy huffed. "Gah! Would you stop peeing? Come on, let's go! At least we can start toward the coast."

Stryker watched the boy head toward the dry home between the boulders. After a moment, he followed, sniffing the air for the scent of the enemy.

He smelled something else instead.

A familiar scent. And a frightening one.

# CHAPTER 22

As Bo squeezed into the gap between the boulders, he thought about the coded message. He remembered the words, but the numbers were already getting a little fuzzy.

So he repeated them under his breath as he kicked dirt over the embers of the fire.

"One twenty, thirty-six, seven, seven, ninety-one."

Then he felt silly. Why was he wasting time on this little campfire? Thousands of bombs were falling on the island every day, to say nothing of flamethrowers and grenades!

Still, he tamped down the dirt before heading outside.

He didn't see Lemmai anywhere. He started to whistle, then felt a furry head knock into his hand.

"Oh!" he said, looking down at the dog. "You snuck up on me."

The dog gave him what he would've sworn was a teasing look, then trotted away. Heading to the west—which Bo confirmed with his new compass. So at least they were going toward the Americans.

Though also toward the Japanese. And the battlefield.

Well, he'd worry about that later. First, he needed to find his sister. His sister would know how to deal with the message—and the machine guns.

"Slow down!" he called, hiking after the dog.

Lemmai glanced over his shoulder, then disappeared into the underbrush.

Bo didn't know anything about tracking, but he was pretty sure Lemmai was following a trail.

Every time he caught sight of the dog, Lemmai was sniffing or listening—or sniffing *and* listening.

The ache returned to Bo's feet. His legs felt heavy. His breath turned ragged, and he heard himself repeating the code numbers like a prayer. "One twenty, thirty-six, seven, seven, ninety-one."

The island became a smear of trees and hills, mosquitoes and roots, the crunch of leaves and the sound of shelling. And every so often, the glimpse of a furry bottom through the trees, urging him onward.

The rumble of battle echoed through the jungle—guns, shells, grenades—getting louder and louder as Bo climbed, until he couldn't tell the bombs from his own heartbeat.

He fell into a daze again, struggling onward while his mind focused on the one thing that mattered.

Find his sister.

Pass along the message.

Tell the Americans about the machine guns surrounding the camp.

Bo surprised himself with a laugh. He could

almost hear Teresita's voice in his head saying, *That's three things.*

"But one at a time," he panted out loud.

Then he saw something that made him stop short.

The dog was standing motionless at the top of a shallow ravine. His ears were pricked, and his whole body was focused on the ditch. Like he'd found what he'd been looking for.

Relief washed over Bo. *The Americans!* It had to be!

A smile spread across his face. Either a marine squad was hiding out of sight or this ravine would lead right to them!

He bustled forward, peering into the ravine. It didn't look like anything special. Just another jungle ditch, lined with rain-flattened grass and dripping bushes. His smile died. Nobody was hiding there, and it sure didn't look like the way toward *anything*.

Another dead end.

"What are you doing?" he asked the dog. "This isn't the way to deliver your message!"

The dog edged closer to a heap of clothing in the dirt.

"I don't need more muddy clothes!" Bo told him. "Look at me! The only thing I *have* is muddy clothes."

The dog kept trotting forward.

"What are you doing?" Bo demanded again.

Then the clothes moved.

A groan sounded, and a filthy hand appeared.

Bo's heart almost burst from his chest in surprise. That wasn't a heap of clothing. That was a *person*!

A marine! The wounded soldier had red hair and a bloody gash on his forehead.

"Hey, pup," he groaned at Lemmai.

"Um," Bo said, warily approaching. "Are you—"

The marine rolled onto his side. Blood covered his arm, but he lifted his pistol quickly enough, pointing directly at Bo—until Stryker bounded between them.

"Wait!" Bo yelped. "Wait, no!"

The red-haired marine lowered his gun.

"You're just a kid."

"I'm Bo."

"Private Mitchum."

"Oh, hi! Are you okay? Do you know Lemmai? I mean, the dog?"

"We've met," the man said, and closed his eyes.

"I found him in the river," Bo said. "He had a message around his collar. It's gone now, but I read it, and I can tell you what it said. Except it's in Chamorro, and I'm not sure if I'm translating it right. And I need to find my sister. The Japanese rounded everyone up and forced us into this camp in the jungle and it's surrounded by machine guns and if you don't stop them, I think—I think they're going to start shooting."

The man didn't respond.

"Hey!" Bo frowned. "Did you hear me?"

The man still didn't respond.

In fact, he didn't move.

Bo looked closer, his stomach twisting.

The marine wasn't breathing!

# CHAPTER 23

Stryker sniffed the wounded marine. That's what he'd smelled earlier: an injured pack-mate. That's why he'd brought the boy here.

The man's head was bleeding. So were his arm and his side. Now he'd fallen still and almost silent. Stryker heard the faintest wheeze of his breath and the weak flutter of his heart. The marine had lost too much blood; if he fell asleep he might never wake.

So Stryker helped him. He roughly licked the wound on the man's head, hard enough to hurt—

cleaning the marine, but also rousing him.

The man groaned and weakly tried to push Stryker away.

"Stop!" the boy snapped at Stryker. "Don't do that!"

Stryker licked the wound again. That time the man pushed him more strongly. Good. He wasn't going to fade away.

"Puppy," the man whispered, his eyes still closed. "Didn't I tell you . . . there's no time for kisses?"

Stryker looked expectantly at the worried boy standing above them. A packmate was in trouble! A human packmate needed human help!

"Okay, okay," the boy said, taking a breath. "Um, we need to get you to a doctor or something."

The man opened his eyes to look at the boy, then closed them again.

"Stay awake!" the boy said, crouching over the man. "Hey, you! Mitchum!"

"You're a pest," the man breathed. "Just like that dog."

"Too bad!" The boy grabbed the man's arm

and tried to pull him to his feet. "I'm going to pester you all the way back to the army!"

With the boy's help, the man pushed weakly to his knees. "No, you won't."

"I will too!"

"You'll pester me . . ." On his third try, the man rose to his feet, draping his arm across the boy's narrow shoulders. ". . . back to the *marines*."

The boy held the man's hand tightly. "First we get you to a doctor."

"Field hospital," the man mumbled.

"Lemmai!" The boy looked at Stryker. "Find the hospital!"

"I know . . . where it is," the man said, and nodded along the ravine.

"Thank God. Lemmai keeps leading me in the wrong direction."

"He brought you to . . . *me*."

"Oh, yeah. I guess that was okay."

The boy and the man started shuffling along. They moved slowly and unsteadily, but they made progress.

Stryker ranged in front of them despite his hurt leg, checking for ambushes. He kept his senses alert for danger, for traps, and for Epstein.

He still had a message to deliver.

The light-haired marine pointed the way along the ravine, then up a rocky hillside. The humans took forever to climb it. They crawled. The man almost fainted. The boy cried in frustration.

As they walked, the chatter of machine guns grew louder. Taunting voices called and grenades exploded.

A cloud of smoke swirled on the breeze, and Stryker smelled the salty tang of the beach. He smelled the blood and sweat of hundreds of men. They were close to base.

The light-haired marine kept sagging. But no matter how many times he faltered, Stryker's boy urged him onward. That boy was as loyal as a dog. Stryker didn't know any higher compliment than that, and—

He smelled Epstein!

The scent wafted around him on a breeze, then faded into the bite of gun smoke and the musk of sweat. Still, Stryker wanted to bark with satisfaction. He'd found Epstein!

He backtracked to the sluggish humans and

almost nipped their heels to encourage them. Hurry up! He knew where to find the scent now!

In the end, he just circled the humans a few times. Walking around on two legs was ridiculous. Stryker didn't know how they even balanced.

Well, the light-haired man wasn't balancing much right then. He leaned more heavily on the boy. His blood soaked his clothes and splattered the ground.

He didn't fall asleep, though. Probably because the boy kept yapping at him, pestering him. Good boy.

"So, um, where are you from?" the boy asked.

"Ohio," the man said.

"No, seriously."

The man's grimace of pain turned into a twisted grin. "Seriously. Ohio."

"That's a place in America?"

"It's a state."

"You're kidding! There's a state named after what you say when someone surprises you? 'Oh! Hi. Oh!'"

"I . . . never thought of it like that."

"Is that how you greet people in Ohio?" the

boy asked. "Oh! Hiyo!"

"If I ever get back home"—the marine panted—"it will be."

Stryker herded them toward Epstein. Through a charred row of trees, past a crater filled with rainwater—then he smelled the enemy.

When he alerted the humans, they fell silent and watched him.

Stryker pointed his snout toward the enemy. He waited until the humans fell into line behind him, then slunk in the opposite direction, keeping one ear cocked.

He was so close to Epstein! He barely even felt his injured leg any longer.

The light-haired marine smelled weaker than ever. Still, he stayed on his feet with the boy's help.

Stryker led his people in a careful, winding route through the thick of the enemy—toward Epstein.

As they climbed the hill, Stryker heard a few enemy soldiers to his left, on the other side of a leafy ridge. He smelled even more of them to the right, hidden in a hollow. They were still a minute's run away, but a big pack was gathering.

Stryker led his people along the safest route through thickets and around pillboxes, scrambling past charred shrubs and over fallen trees. Finally, they left the enemy behind.

"How about . . . you?" the light-haired marine asked, his voice soft from caution—or weakness. "Where are you from? New York?"

"Of course not! I'm from Guam. I'm from *here*!" The boy made a face. "Oh, you're kidding."

"It must've been rough . . . during the occupation. Even for a kid as tough as you."

"I'm not tough."

"Not tough?" The marine stopped walking until the boy looked at his face. "You appeared out of the jungle with . . . with fire in your eyes and a war dog at your heels. You're the kind of tough they write stories about."

"I'm not! I'm scared all the time! I'm just doing the best I can."

"Kid," the marine said. "That's what tough *is*."

# CHAPTER 24

"**O**ne twenty, thirty-six, seven—" Bo followed the dog, repeating the code numbers under his breath.

There was a sudden rustling of leaves. Before Bo could react, a dozen hard-eyed men in dirty uniforms stalked from the jungle. Bo would've fainted, but he didn't want to drop Private Mitchum.

Also, the men were Americans.

After a tense moment, they recognized Mitchum's uniform.

"What're you doing here?" one asked. "Who's the kid?"

"Who's the *dog*?" another asked.

Bo interrupted them. "He needs the hospital."

"I got . . . separated," Mitchum said, as a medic jogged forward. "The kid helped . . ."

Like a furry flash, Stryker raced between the marines toward a curly-haired man who was stepping from the jungle. Giving a single bark, Stryker sat at the man's feet.

"Stryker!" The marine scratched the dog's head, then reached for his collar. "You've got a message?"

"Um," Bo said.

The marine frowned at Stryker. "He's hurt!"

"He got a little shot. I put ointment on him . . ." Bo trailed off when the marine took the tube from the collar. "Er, the message is gone."

"Gone? How?"

"I read it, though. I memorized it."

"Well, what did it say?"

"It's in Chamorro."

The marine rubbed Stryker's ears. "What's a Chamorro?"

"It's our language. What we speak in Guam."

"Oh! Right." The marine turned his head and shouted. "Hey, Santos! Santos, we need someone who speaks Guamian!"

"I'm right here, Epstein," a dark-haired marine said, pushing into the opening. "And it's still not called Guamian."

"You're Chamorro," Bo said to the new guy.

"So are you," Santos said, hunkering down in front of Bo. "You've got a message?"

"You're a marine! And Chamorro!"

"Yeah."

"Chamorro *and* a marine," Bo said.

Santos grinned. "That's right, kid. What's the message?"

"Oh. Right. Um." Bo repeated the message and the numbers. "I'm pretty sure that's what it said."

Santos translated the message into English for the rest of the marines. "The Japanese are attacking from both sides," Santos finished. "They're making one big final push, once they get in place. And we were supposed to know about this *yesterday*."

"They're already in place," Mitchum said,

as the medic bandaged his head. "They're three hundred yards away, maybe a little more. The dog led us past them."

There was a flurry of conversation about military stuff that Bo didn't understand. Epstein called Stryker to check his wounds. The dog gave Bo a look over his shoulder and trotted away.

The marines surged into action, preparing for the attack. Bo was swept along with them, toward freshly dug ditches and a captured concrete pillbox.

"Um, excuse me?" he said to the nearest marine. "There are machine guns around the Chamorros—"

"There are machine guns everywhere."

"No, I mean halfway across the island."

The marine grunted. "Then they're the best kind of guns—the ones we don't have to worry about."

"But they're surrounding the—"

"Keep your head down," the marine said, and trotted off.

Bo sidled toward Mitchum, but the medic shooed him away with a bloody bandage. So he looked for Epstein. He needed to tell someone about the machine guns around the Chamorro encampment!

"Um, excuse me?" he said.

"There you are!" Epstein grabbed his arm. "You need to get out of here, kid."

"Would you *listen* to me? I saw the Japanese with machine guns and, and—I need to find my sister!"

"Your sister?"

"She's the one who wrote the message."

"That's some family," Epstein said.

"*She'll* make someone listen," Bo said.

Epstein offered him the end of a leash. "Take Stryker. He'll lead you away before the Japanese hit. If you're still here when they attack, we can't protect you. Get moving!"

Bo took the leash. "Who do I tell about—"

"And take Mitchum too," Epstein said.

"I'm staying," Mitchum said, even though he looked worse than ever, his red hair hidden by a fresh bandage.

"That's an order," another marine told him. "Bring the kid to the field hospital. You can't hardly move your legs, but you'll make it that far."

"I don't need my legs, just my trigger finger."

Bo knelt in front of the dog as the marines argued. "Stryker? That's your name?"

Stryker perked his ears, listening for new dangers among the thunder of shelling.

"You still look like a Lemmai to me," Bo told him.

"Kid!" the one named Epstein shouted. "Time to go. *Now!*"

"C'mere." Mitchum stretched out one arm almost like a hug. "Are you up to being my crutch again?"

"Sure thing," Bo said.

Mitchum leaned his weight on Bo, and Epstein snapped commands to Stryker, telling him to find the hospital.

Stryker led them away, and after they took twenty steps Bo unhooked the leash. He felt safer with Stryker on the loose.

Mitchum watched but didn't say anything. Maybe he *couldn't* say anything. Despite his earlier bravado, his breathing sounded weak and raspy, and he shuffled more than he walked.

The path downhill was slippery with leaves. Branches scratched Bo's face and snagged Mitchum's uniform. Apparently the hospital was near the beach, through a patch of jungle, and—

Behind him, the Japanese attacked.

# CHAPTER 25

When the boy unclipped the leash, Stryker didn't even look back. He knew the boy would follow. They were bound together by something stronger than a length of rope.

And when the enemy attacked the marines behind them, he didn't bother swiveling his ears.

Still, the crackle of gunfire and the *thwoom* of explosions thumped in his chest.

A thin shriek made his skin itch.

He didn't slow, though. He'd delivered his

message; that job was done. Now he had a new mission. He needed to lead the boy and the wounded light-haired marine to safety, to the tent called "hospital" where his wounded packmates gathered.

Stryker chose the path over the ridge and then downhill toward the beach, favoring his injured leg. He zigged to the left, away from an exposed treeless knoll, then waited for the humans to catch up. He zagged to the right, away from a patch of earth that stank of acrid explosive and harsh metal: a land mine.

The underbrush abruptly ended. He caught a glimpse of the ocean and turned away, waiting for the boy and man to reach him.

The boy looked drawn but determined. The man looked half-dead.

Somehow, they stayed on their feet.

At the bottom of the hill, an explosion deafened Stryker.

His ears buzzed like a thousand bees. He shook his head, but the silence remained. He still smelled shattered wood and overturned earth, but he heard nothing.

He shook himself again.

A faint hum sounded. The barest whisper of explosions. He smelled the boy and man move noiselessly beside him. He felt the boy's hand in his fur; he felt his warmth and his trust.

Stryker leaned against the boy's skinny leg. Together, they picked their way through the brush toward the sharp, chemical smell of the hospital. He didn't need his hearing: the scents would guide him.

His nostrils flaring, he trotted through a smoky stretch of jungle and past abandoned foxholes. The ringing in his ears faded, and the racket of the world returned, engines roaring and machines grunting.

And there! The scent of the wounded. The antiseptic stink of bandages and medicine filled the air. Stryker pushed forward.

"The field hospital," the boy said, heading for the urgent chatter of the doctors and the sobbing of injured men.

The light-haired man groaned in reply.

"Almost there," the boy said. "One more minute."

Stryker heard urgency in the boy's voice—and Mitchum's weight collapsed on his narrow shoulders.

# CHAPTER 26

**B**o almost wept with frustration. He couldn't keep Mitchum on his feet!

But he refused to fall. He gritted his teeth, his arms burning and his legs trembling— and Mitchum somehow found the strength to straighten.

When Bo spotted the field hospital through a cloud of smoke, his heart almost burst with relief.

"We're here!" he told Mitchum.

Mitchum gritted his teeth and took one more step.

Bo's back ached from bearing the marine's weight. Still, he held him tight. Mitchum shuffled one more step. Then another.

As they staggered onward, Bo felt Mitchum's determination in his wiry, exhausted body. He felt Mitchum force himself forward by willpower alone.

Somehow, that gave Bo strength. That and Stryker's endless courage and energy. The dog never wavered. He'd crossed through enemy territory without hesitation, leading Bo and Mitchum to safety.

Except Stryker suddenly stopped, his ears pricking at some sound.

Bo's blood ran cold. He knew that look; he knew it meant trouble.

Before he could react, two marines jogged toward them, carrying a stretcher for Mitchum. Stryker didn't respond to them, he just peered into the distance. The danger was farther away. The marines spared a glance at Bo, but they were too focused on Mitchum to pay him much attention.

In a flash, they were carrying the wounded

marine into the field hospital. Bo tagged along, rubbing his own aching shoulders and wondering what had alarmed Stryker.

Inside the tent, dozens of wounded soldiers lay on the cots lining the walls. Everywhere Bo looked, he saw another bloody bandage or open wound. The air stank of sweat and iodine—and worse.

Bo felt his knees weaken. He almost fainted before he felt a muscular, furry shoulder rubbing against his calf. He took a breath and stroked the fur on Stryker's neck. Okay, now that Mitchum was in the hospital, he needed to find his sister. He needed to ask someone how to find her. He needed—

A sweaty marine burst inside and ran to one of the doctors. Bo frowned as they talked in urgent undertones. What was that about? What was happening? First Stryker had pricked up his ears, and now *this*.

"Hey, kid!" one of the stretcher bearers called. "Your buddy wants you."

Bo crossed the field hospital to stand beside Mitchum. "Are you okay?"

"Epstein said . . ." Mitchum pulled himself higher on his cot. "If you tell the pup, 'Report to Dawson,' . . . he'll take you to his handler."

"He will?"

"But you have to say it firm, like a command," Mitchum continued. "And his handler will know where that message came from."

"You mean—"

"The one your sister wrote. He'll know where your sister is."

"Oh, thank God!" Bo felt jittery with relief. "I'll tell her everything. Then she'll tell the Americans—the marines! And I'll come back here, I promise, I'll—"

"The Japanese broke through!" the sweaty marine shouted. "They're coming this way. And if they get past us, they'll be in position to retake the entire peninsula."

A hubbub erupted in the field hospital. One of the doctors started handing rifles and pistols to injured patients. Bandaged marines who'd looked like they couldn't raise their heads suddenly pushed themselves from their cots and checked their weapons. Bo watched wide-eyed until

Mitchum grabbed his arm and roared, "Scram! Bo, *now.* Call the pup and run, before they get here!"

Bo didn't ask any questions, he didn't hesitate. He just obeyed.

"Stryker!" he shouted, running toward the tent flap. "Come!"

He raced outside. Mortar shells exploded fifty feet away, digging chunks out of the earth. He could hear the crack of nearby rifles and the chatter of machine guns moving in their direction.

Bo dove behind a fallen tree. A heartbeat later, Stryker slammed into him and the two of them crouched there, barely hidden from the enemy.

He could hear the howls of the Japanese soldiers as they made their way toward the field hospital. The crashing and shrieking reminded him of that wild boar attacking Two Ears in the jungle.

Bo felt himself tremble. Okay. He got scared. So what? He'd stay scared, but he'd do his best. Like Mitchum said, that's what tough *was.*

Stryker nudged Bo's blood-smeared arm. Huh. Maybe even Stryker got scared.

"Don't worry, boy," Bo whispered. "I'm right here."

Stryker nudged him again, and Bo felt his heart break for this loyal, brave dog . . . and for himself. He'd never reach his sister, not now. Not with so many troops swarming onto the hospital grounds. He'd never see his parents again. He'd never warn the Americans about those machine guns.

Still, he needed to stay strong for Stryker.

"I-I'll take care of you," Bo said in a shaky voice.

A splatter of bullets ripped across the other side of the tree, shredding the wood into splinters.

The enemy forces were too close. Grenades exploded, and screams tore the air. The big navy guns boomed in response from the ships off the shore.

A star shell burst in the early evening sky, casting a harsh light down on the battlefield.

Stryker snarled as the Japanese soldiers rushed toward the fallen tree hiding them.

Bo grabbed a branch from the ground. "W-we almost made it," he told the dog, tightening his grip. "We almost made it."

Stryker growled again.

Bo hunkered down and braced himself.

"You and me," Bo said, tears in his eyes. "Together till the end."

# CHAPTER 27

For one heartbeat, Bo thought he was dead. Then he realized that the bullets were coming from *behind* him. From the field hospital.

He looked over his shoulder and gasped at the sight.

The wounded marines were fighting off the Japanese. A bunch of men covered in bloody bandages leaned against makeshift barricades, holding rifles. Others on crutches aimed a mortar, a portable tube for launching bombs.

A shock of red hair poked out from under one

of the rifleman's bandages. It was Mitchum! He bellowed at Bo, but his words were lost in the gunfire.

Still, Bo understood his gestures. He was showing Bo how to escape!

As the wounded marines held off the Japanese attack, Bo crawled in the direction Mitchum had indicated, away from the firefight.

Stryker stayed with Bo, guarding his back as they wormed along behind a fallen tree, then crept past a row of crushed bushes to a ditch a few hundred yards away.

Together, they followed the ditch as the battle raged behind them.

Bo almost fainted from relief and exhaustion when they climbed from the muddy trench, far from the chaos. Instead, he wiped dirt from his face and said, "Hey, Stryker."

The dog kept gazing toward the fight. His coat twitched in a way that meant he was listening.

"Report," Bo said. "Report to Dawson."

Stryker spun toward him, his eyes brightening and his ears pricking up. His dirty, stubby tail wagged happily, and Bo was pretty sure that he *smiled*.

Despite his aches and fatigue, Bo laughed. "Go on, Lemmai. Find Dawson."

Stryker gave him one last grin, then started trotting along a wide dirt path.

Bo followed until they came to the outskirts of the American base. A minute later, a bunch of marines ran past. They looked like they were heading toward the field hospital to reinforce the troops. One of them almost tripped when he saw Bo, who must've looked like a ball of mud with legs.

Other marines called out questions as Bo trailed Stryker through their camp, but he didn't stop to answer. He was afraid he'd lose Stryker.

He shouldn't have worried, because even from across the camp he would've heard the man yell, "*Stryker!*"

Stryker took off ahead. He flashed past a mound of engine parts and into a field of tents. Bo jogged between the tents, trying to keep sight of Stryker's tail. When he raced around a corner, he saw a marine on his knees outside a low tent, hugging Stryker.

"I thought I'd lost you, buddy," the marine said in a choked voice. "I thought I'd lost you."

Stryker wagged his tail like a puppy and licked tears from the marine's face. So that was Dawson.

After a minute, Dawson noticed Bo standing beside him and jerked in surprise. Then he shook his head. "For a second, you looked like my little brother, Matt." He grinned. "After falling into a swamp. Are you okay? Do you—" He looked between Stryker and Bo. "Oh. Stryker knows you."

"Yeah, um, I brought him across the island. I mean, *he* brought *me*. Well, I guess we brought each other."

Dawson whistled, still hugging Stryker. "That sounds like some story. All the way across the island? You look beat, kid. Sit down and I'll see if—"

"Thanks but, um—Epstein said that you know my sister?"

"Miss Cruz?"

Bo nodded. "Yeah. Carmen. I'm her brother, Bo."

"I knew you looked familiar!" Dawson glanced at Stryker. He must've wanted to clean him and tend to him—but whatever he saw in Stryker's face made him look back to Bo. "Let's find your sister."

"Please! Yes. Thank you."

Dawson rummaged in his pack as he led Bo across the camp. "I bet you're hungry."

"Starving. Stryker ate all the fruit we found."

"Greedy dog," Dawson said, and gave Bo a chocolate bar.

"*Dangkulu na si Yu'us ma'ase,*" Bo said. *Thank you very much.*

"Um, *boon prochebu?*" Dawson said, heading past one of the larger tents. "Is that right? Your sister taught me how to say 'you're welcome,' but I'm sure I got it wrong."

He'd gotten it completely wrong, but Bo liked that he'd tried. "Nah," he said, "That's perfect."

"So where did you find Stry—"

"Bo!" Carmen raced past a startled marine and swept Bo into her arms. "Bo, Bo! What are you *doing* here? Where's Dad? You should have stayed with Dad! I'm so glad to see you! Look at you! You're filthy! You're embarrassing me in front of the marines." She hugged him tight and started crying. "Thank God you're okay!"

"You—you need to tell them!" he said, wiping tears from his own eyes when she released him.

"Tell who what?"

"The officers!" Bo said. "Tell them that the Japanese herded us into a camp in the middle of the jungle. They're surrounding thousands of Chamorros with machine guns!"

Carmen's smile faded. She looked at Dawson over Bo's shoulder. "Did you hear that? We need to tell someone."

"The colonel," Dawson said. "C'mon. This way."

He led them into a big tent bustling with marines. Scary, important, *busy* marines. "Colonel," he said to an older marine. "This is Bo. There's something you need to hear."

Bo suddenly felt very small and very young. Still, he said, "Sir?"

The older marine glanced at Bo. "Get this kid somewhere safe."

"No," Bo said. "You need to listen to me!"

The old marine looked closer at the brave, grimy boy standing there with a brave, grimy war dog at his side.

"Y'know," the old man said. "Maybe I do."

And Bo told his story, standing straight and unafraid.

# EPILOGUE

TWO WEEKS LATER

**A**fter the day's second patrol, Dawson led Stryker toward the veterinary tent.

Halfway there, Stryker caught the scent. His heart leaped in his chest, and he dashed in an excited circle.

"Yeah," Dawson thumped his side. "I feel exactly the same."

Inside the tent, Stryker strained at his leash. He gave a few playful barks even though he knew he wasn't supposed to. He dashed past Ramirez and lowered onto his chest with his butt in the air, inviting Boomer to chase.

Because Boomer was alive! He smelled weak, but he was *alive*.

When Stryker barked again, Boomer huffed at him. The bigger dog was too well behaved to bark . . . but his tail wagged wildly.

Stryker sniffed his packmate.

Boomer sniffed back.

Stryker gave him a sidelong look. *Poor sluggish Boomer. Too slow to dodge a bullet.*

Boomer tilted his nose in the air. *Poor Stryker, too weak to shrug off a bullet.*

After a happy flop of his tongue, Stryker rubbed his head against his friend. Boomer licked Stryker's muzzle.

Then everything got even better.

Stryker's boy stepped inside the tent, followed by another human child. And the boy was holding a delicious-smelling pot.

"How'd you get in here?" Dawson asked Bo. "They give you the run of the camp?"

"He's our lucky charm," Ramirez said.

"This is my friend Teresita," Bo told the men. "That's Dawson and Ramirez."

"You can call me Eric," Dawson told Teresita. "Nice to meet you."

She shook his hand. "You're the marine with the dog!"

"And you're the girl Bo met in the camp?"

She nodded. "Yeah."

"How are your sisters?"

"Better now. Thanks to the marines. You got there just in time to save us."

"After Bo told us what was happening. He's the real hero."

"Eh, he just did one thing," the girl said, nudging Bo with her elbow.

Stryker's boy flushed with pleasure. He raised his pot of food. "My mom sent us with this. It's red rice. For Mitchum."

"That lucky dog," Ramirez muttered as he patted Boomer.

Stryker and Boomer licked and nuzzled each other while the people talked. Then Dawson led the boy and girl away, to the *other* veterinary tent. The one for humans.

"Oh!" Bo said, setting his food down beside the light-haired marine.

The light-haired marine smiled. "Hi."

"Oh!" Bo finished, with a laugh.

The marine clasped Bo's hand. They didn't say anything, but Stryker understood: they were packmates.

"These are the guys who stopped the Japanese attack," Bo told the girl. "A bunch of injured marines, the walking wounded, held off the enemy."

"That was the end of the line for the Japanese," Dawson said.

"Really?" the girl asked, looking around, wide-eyed. "That's when you won?"

"Well, it's not completely over yet," Dawson said. "We're still mopping up a few Japanese hiding on the island."

"With all the caves and jungle nooks," the light-haired marine said, "we have to make sure we get all of them."

"Luckily we have war dogs to root them out," Dawson said. "That's our next mission. Clearing caves and tracking the enemy through the jungle."

"Good puppies," the light-haired marine said.

"There should be statues to them," the boy said.

"What about you, Bo?" the light-haired marine asked. "Do you want a statue?"

"Nah," the boy said. "The only thing I ever wanted was a banana."

Stryker didn't understand the words, but the humans' laughter pleased him.

He let the warmth soak into him, the fondness and friendship. His stumpy tail wagged with happiness. He enjoyed every scrap of affection, like licking meat off a bone.

Because these were the moments marines lived for. These were the moments they *fought* for.

# DID DOGS LIKE STRYKER REALLY SERVE DURING WORLD WAR II?

**Y**up! When the war broke out, many Americans wanted to help—including the furry ones. Families across the country donated their dogs to a group called Dogs for Defense, who trained the brave pups to do important military tasks.

In boot camp, canine trainees learned to search for folks lost in fires and under rubble, carry cables and supplies, and alert their handlers to enemy sneak attacks. They were taught to respond to spoken commands like "FIND!" and "ATTACK!"

The character of Stryker was inspired by the Dobermans of World War II who served alongside the US Marines!

# TIMELINE OF GUAM

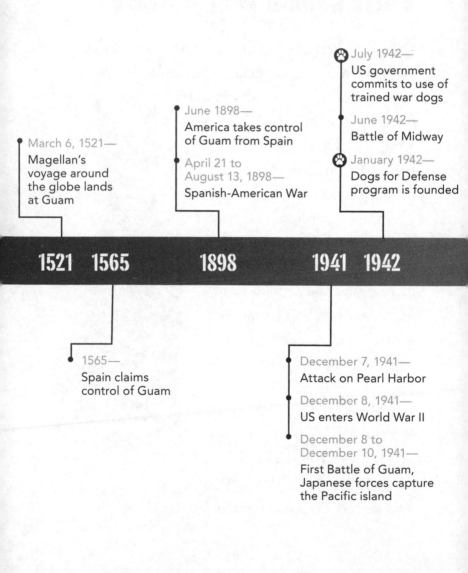

July 1942—
US government commits to use of trained war dogs

June 1942—
Battle of Midway

January 1942—
Dogs for Defense program is founded

June 1898—
America takes control of Guam from Spain

April 21 to August 13, 1898—
Spanish-American War

March 6, 1521—
Magellan's voyage around the globe lands at Guam

## 1521   1565        1898        1941   1942

1565—
Spain claims control of Guam

December 7, 1941—
Attack on Pearl Harbor

December 8, 1941—
US enters World War II

December 8 to December 10, 1941—
First Battle of Guam, Japanese forces capture the Pacific island

# AND THE PACIFIC FRONT:

September 2, 1945—
V-J Day (Victory in Japan), Japanese sign surrender agreement

August 14, 1945 —
Japanese forces surrender

August 9, 1945—
Atomic bomb dropped on Nagasaki

August 6, 1945—
Atomic bomb dropped on Hiroshima

February to March 1945—
Battle of Iwo Jima

July 21, 1994—
50th anniversary of victory on Guam; memorial statue dedicated

**1944  1945**                    **1972**       **1994**

June 6, 1944—
D-Day at Normandy in France

July 21 to
August 8, 1944—
Second Battle of Guam; US takes control from Japan

October 1944—
Battle of Leyte Gulf

January 24, 1972—
Last World War II Japanese soldier found hiding on Guam

# Q&A ABOUT THE SECOND BATTLE OF GUAM

**Q. Who are the Chamorros?**

A. Chamorros are the native or indigenous people who live throughout the Mariana Islands, the chain of islands in the North Pacific Ocean that includes Guam and Saipan. They first settled the area over seven thousand years ago and have a complex and rich culture. Their traditions have been challenged by a history of colonization—when outside countries came and claimed their land as their own.

**Q. Why do many of the Chamorro people in the book have Spanish-sounding names?**

A. Guam was first colonized by Spain in the sixteenth century. Because of this, many people on Guam are Roman Catholic and have names that sound Spanish.

**Q. But Guam is an American territory now, right?**

A. Yes. In 1898, during the Spanish-American

War, the Americans defeated the Spanish and took control of the island. The United States ruled until 1941, when the Japanese attacked during the First Battle of Guam. When the US retook the island after the Second Battle of Guam in 1944, it was declared a US territory.

Like Puerto Rico, the island of Guam is still a US territory instead of a state. This means that they can't vote for the president, and their congressperson can't vote on laws in the House of Representatives. The US military still controls almost a third of the land on the island and many people, including the United Nations, believe the island should be returned to its native people as its own country.

**Q. When did the Japanese navy invade Guam? Why Guam?**

A. The Japanese didn't waste any time after bombing Pearl Harbor. They invaded Guam the very next day, December 8, 1941, in an attack now called the First Battle of Guam. They quickly took control of the island from the Americans and renamed it Omiya Jima, which means "Great

Shrine Island" in Japanese. Guam was a lot closer geographically to Japan than any other American territory. Since bomber planes couldn't make the journey across the entire Pacific Ocean, this kept American planes from flying from Guam to Japan to attack.

**Q. What was the Japanese military rule like for natives of Guam?**
A. In a word, bad. Many people died in the invasion of the island. Chamorro people who were suspected of helping the American cause were arrested, tortured, and killed. Some families tried to hide their children from the Japanese. But many Chamorros ended up in concentration camps or hard labor camps like the one Bo was sent to.

**Q. Were code talkers really used during the Battle of Guam?**
A. The famous code talkers of World War II were Navajo servicemen, mostly marines, who used their native language to help American forces send secret messages. The Navajo language was so difficult to learn that their code was unbreakable

and led to several major American victories in the Pacific theater! There isn't any official record of Chamorro people working as code talkers, but some of the Navajos were on Guam during the battle there in 1944.

# WHO WERE THE DOBERMANS OF WORLD WAR II?

The Dobermans of World War II were a highly trained group of dogs who served with the US Marines in combat between the years 1942 and 1945. They carried supplies, delivered messages, scouted for enemies, and protected military camps.

Each dog trained closely with a specific handler who was also a marine. The close bond between handler and dog made sure that the dogs would do anything to protect their person. And the dogs' strong sense of smell made it possible to find their handlers when delivering messages, even from a long way away. They were also able to smell enemy forces and warn their people about ambushes!

Dobermans were also used to "mop up" the island after the war. They searched all the jungle caves on the island to find any enemy soldiers who had gone into hiding. Even then they missed a few: the last Japanese straggler wasn't discovered until 1972. He'd been hiding in the jungle for twenty-eight years and believed the war was still going on!

The brave soldier dogs who gave their lives during the Second Battle of Guam were so helpful to the war effort that a memorial was built to celebrate them in 1994 at the US Naval Base in Guam. A statue of Kurt, one of the real-life hero dogs of Guam, sits on top of the memorial. Kurt and another Doberman named Rex inspired the character of Stryker!

# TOP TEN FACTS ABOUT THE DOBERMANS OF WORLD WAR II

**1.** Dobermans can bite down with between 200–400 pounds of force—enough to break a person's arm!

**2.** Dobermans are very easy to train. They're the fifth-smartest breed of dog!

**3.** Dobermans are usually about two and a half feet tall and weigh around 100 pounds.

**4.** Dobermans were one of seven breeds chosen as the best candidates for the Dogs for Defense program.

**5.** Dobermans and other dogs were trained at the marines' Camp Lejeune in North Carolina.

**6.** A total of 549 Doberman war dogs served on Guam.

**7.** Most of the Dobermans who served on Guam were successfully retrained and returned to their families after the war.

**8.** Some dogs were later adopted by their handlers instead.

**9.** The marine Dobermans were nicknamed Devil Dogs.

**10.** Even though dogs couldn't receive the same military awards as people, some Dobermans were so brave their people still recommended they get military honors.

# PACIFIC FRONT Q&A

**Q. What are D-rations?**
A. Short answer: chocolate! During World War II, the Hershey Company designed special chocolate bars that didn't melt. They were called Tropical Chocolate Bars because most of them went to the troops on the Pacific front.

**Q. How can something be a car AND a boat?**
A. The car-boats that Stryker sees at the American camps are called DUKWs. They're amphibious (just like frogs!). These flat-bottomed boats with wheels carried troops and gear from a big ship straight onto dry land and kept going!

**Q. What are Japanese Yonkis?**

A. *Yonki* means four-wheel drive in Japanese. It was also a nickname for the Kurogane-brand jeeps popular with the Japanese military. Around 4,700 of them were used during World War II!

**Q. What were pillboxes?**

A. Pillboxes were concrete shelters used by Japanese forces to protect themselves from machine gun fire. Japanese fighters made the Chamorros set up defenses like pillboxes before the second battle on Guam. The Americans had to use trenches and foxholes—narrow, deep holes that a whole person could hide in—to stay out of enemy fire while fighting back.

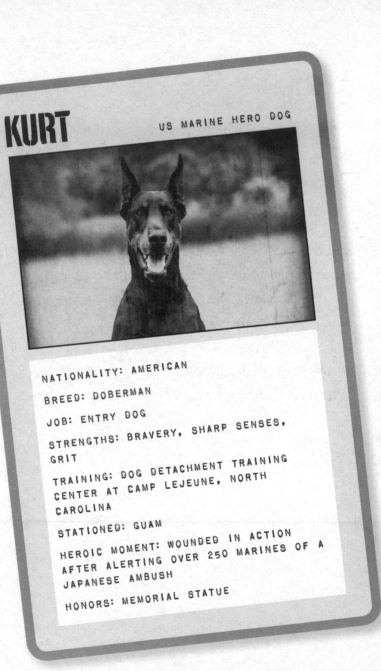

# KURT

US MARINE HERO DOG

NATIONALITY: AMERICAN

BREED: DOBERMAN

JOB: ENTRY DOG

STRENGTHS: BRAVERY, SHARP SENSES, GRIT

TRAINING: DOG DETACHMENT TRAINING CENTER AT CAMP LEJEUNE, NORTH CAROLINA

STATIONED: GUAM

HEROIC MOMENT: WOUNDED IN ACTION AFTER ALERTING OVER 250 MARINES OF A JAPANESE AMBUSH

HONORS: MEMORIAL STATUE

# REX

NATIONALITY: AMERICAN

BREED: DOBERMAN

JOB: SCOUT DOG

STRENGTHS: INTELLIGENCE, BRAVERY, LOYALTY

TRAINING: DOG DETACHMENT TRAINING CENTER AT CAMP LEJEUNE, NORTH CAROLINA

STATIONED: BOUGAINVILLE ISLAND

HEROIC MOMENT: WARNING HIS PLATOON ABOUT A JAPANESE AMBUSH

HONORS: COMMENDATION FROM HIS COMMANDING OFFICER

# Join the Fight!

DON'T MISS THE NEXT
ACTION—PACKED MISSION

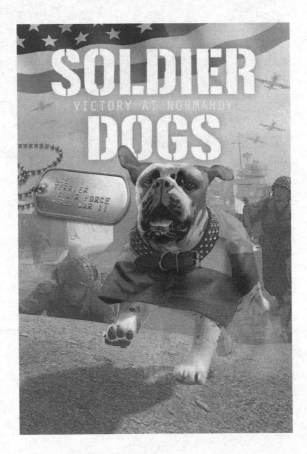

The light flickered both on the ground and in the air. And in those flashes, shapes could be seen—planes flying low, fortresses on the beach, men hanging from parachutes that billowed over them like mushroom caps.

The storm of battle.

The first rumblings of what would be one of the longest days the world would ever know.

As Henri and Elle ran for their lives, every second felt like a hundred years. Ace, the energetic Boston terrier separated from his American soldier handlers, bounded at their side. Behind them, merging with the rumbling of artillery, they could hear the throaty barking of larger dogs— Nazi Dobermans, running after them with teeth bared.

*We have to outrun them*, thought Henri. *If we don't, the war might be lost.*

The war had seen empires rise and cities fall. Germany had taken countless countries. The Allied nations standing against Hitler had been bombed and battered. Now, they were ready to take back the world.

# Love dogs?
## You may also like...